MW01195378

ELIZABETH
THE HIGHLAND CLAN BOOK 12
Published by Keira Montclair
Copyright © 2021 by Keira Montclair

All rights reserved. Except for use in any review, the reproduction or utilization of this work in whole or in part in any form by any electronic, mechanical or other means, now known or hereinafter invented, including xerography, photocopying and recording, or in any information storage or retrieval system, is forbidden without the written permission of the publisher.

This is a work of fiction. Names, characters, places and incidents are either the product of the author's imagination or are used fictitiously, and any resemblance to actual persons, living or dead, business establishments, events or locales is entirely coincidental.

Printed in the USA.

Cover Design and Interior Format

KEIRA
BESTSELLING AUTHOR
MONTCLAIR

THE GRANTS AND RAMSAYS *in 1290s*

GRANTS

LAIRD ALEXANDER GRANT and wife, MADDIE
John (Jake) and wife, Aline—son, Alasdair
James (Jamie) and wife, Gracie—sons, Elshander, Alaric
Kyla and husband, Finlay—sons, Alick, Broc
Connor and wife, Sela—daughters Claray, Dyna
Elizabeth
Maeve

BRENNA GRANT and husband, QUADE RAMSAY
Torrian (Quade's son from his first marriage) and wife, Heather—Nellie (Heather's daughter from a previous relationship) and son, Lachlan
Lily (Quade's daughter from his first marriage) and husband, Kyle—twin daughters, Lise and Liliana
Bethia and husband, Donnan—son, Drystan
Gregor and wife, Merewen
Jennet
Emma, adopted
Geva, adopted

ROBBIE GRANT and wife, CARALYN
Ashlyn (Caralyn's daughter from a previous relationship) and husband, Magnus—daughter, Isbeil
Gracie (Caralyn's daughter from a previous relationship) and husband, Jamie—son, Elshander
Rodric (Roddy) and wife, Rose
Padraig

BRODIE GRANT and wife, CELESTINA
Loki (adopted) and wife, Arabella—sons, Kenzie (adopted) and Lucas, daughter Ami,
Braden and wife, Cairstine—son Steenie
Catriona
Alison

JENNIE GRANT and husband, AEDAN CAMERON
Tara
Riley
Brin

RAMSAYS

QUADE RAMSAY and wife, BRENNA GRANT (see above)

LOGAN RAMSAY and wife, GWYNETH
Molly (adopted) and husband, Tormod
Maggie (adopted) and husband, Will
Sorcha and husband, Cailean
Gavin and wife, Linnet
Brigid
Simone, adopted
Beatris, adopted

MICHEIL RAMSAY and wife, DIANA
David and wife, Anna
Daniel and wife, Constance
Mariana, adopted
Crisly, adopted

AVELINA RAMSAY and DREW MENZIE
Elyse
Tad
Tomag
Maitland

CHAPTER ONE

Early winter, 1290,
The Highlands of Scotland

GIL GRANT CAME abreast of his comrades, Loki, Kenzie, Thorn, and Nari, outside of the gates of Grant Castle, presently open. They were all in merry moods, having come for one of the Grants' small festivals, which only made the scene they rode into more unexpected.

Utter chaos reigned.

Grant guards were charging out through the open gates, a senseless rush of them, something most irregular for Clan Grant, where the guards were famously well-trained. The lairds, Jake and Jamie Grant, had learned well from their father, Alexander Grant, renowned as the finest swordsman in all of Scotland, and it was they who kept order in this part of the Highlands.

They were usually not the ones to disturb it.

Kenzie looked at Gil and sputtered, "Gillie, what the hell is happening?"

Gil shook his head, though not without fondness. "Every time you get anxious about something, you go back to calling me Gillie. You know I prefer Gil now." They had grown up together, near enough, both of them having joined Clan Grant as orphans. Thorn and Nari too. They'd been taken in by Alex's nephew, Loki, and raised in Castle Curanta, an outpost of the Grants'.

Kenzie rolled his eyes, but his attention shifted back to the show in front of them as Alex's voice carried over the area. Although his words were unclear, he sounded furious.

Loki looked back at the four younger men, wide-eyed, and tugged on the reins of his horse, flying toward the gate just as Alex came out through the portcullis, shoving a man Gil didn't recognize. Connor came barreling after them.

The stranger, dressed in a way that suggested wealth, bellowed back at Alex. Loki leaped from his horse and joined Alex and Connor, while Gil and the others stayed back, dismounting as they watched the scene play out in front of them.

The giant Highland warriors pursued the Englishman, who had recovered enough sense to retreat as four guards dressed in English garb closed in around the bellowing stranger. Everyone knew the English were terrible swordsmen. Did they not realize Clan Grant's warriors numbered over a thousand? Dozens of Grant warriors were already headed their way from the lists, and a single wave of Connor Grant's hand would bring hundreds of men charging faster than an Englishman could mount a horse.

Gil's group stayed back, watching from a distance as the din and the crowd grew.

"What the hell could have happened?" Kenzie whispered.

"Hush," Gil said, holding up a hand, wanting to listen to the conversation.

"How dare you step onto my land and draw blood from my daughter," Alex bellowed. Gil's stomach dropped to his toes. He'd been in love with Alex's daughter, Elizabeth, for quite some time now, though they'd kept their relationship secret by mutual agreement. Given this festival was being held in Lizzie's honor—she was still unmarried, and her parents were actively seeking a partner for her—she had to be the daughter who'd been dishonored. He clenched his fists because he knew he couldn't intervene. Not if he was to keep his word to her.

"I don't know of what you speak," the man replied, crossing his arms, a sly look on his face. From his accent, he was an Englishman.

Elizabeth ran out through the gates next, several more guards coming out with her. "Papa, please leave him be. Send him away and be done with it."

Connor stalked out from behind his father. "I'll kill him first. That will put an end to it." He grabbed the man's leine and lifted him in the air. "You dare to touch my sister? Force her outside without her permission?"

The man laughed and said, "She wanted it. I had her permission and more. You just choose not to believe it. Lizzie will be my wife. Or should I call her Eliza?"

Gil shoved through the crowd to get closer, but Connor already had a grip on the bastard, so there was little he could do. But there was much he'd *like* to do—string him up by his bollocks, cut his throat, have a fist fight with him so he'd have the pleasure of blackening both of the dandy's eyes.

He took his eyes off the bastard and stared at the ground, forcing his emotions back under control. This would be the greatest test of his self-control.

Connor hoisted the man up higher, practically choking him. "No one calls her 'Lizzie.'"

"When she belongs to me, she'll do whatever I tell her to do, and answer to whatever I wish to call her, whether you savage Scots approve or not. Mayhap Beth. Aye, that suits me even better." He grinned, a wicked grin that told more of his personality than anything else he could do. Insulting her and her family to their faces did not bother the bastard at all. Gil clenched his fists over and over again, glad her brothers were here to handle the bastard because he'd be foolish enough to go after him alone and the fool had many guards who would gladly have stopped him.

The man's closest four guards attempted to surround them, causing fifty Grant warriors to unsheathe their swords in unison, the sharp ting of metal echoing in the dark night. The tension between the groups was of the kind Gil had seen before battle.

Gil took two steps toward Elizabeth, his heart now in his throat at the possibility that she'd been hurt. Alex had said blood had been drawn. His gaze caught hers and he scanned her face, noticing the blood on her lower lip, but what upset him more was the way she was visibly trembling.

Elizabeth had a strong constitution. Whatever had happened, it must have been a major affront to have affected her so. But he couldn't touch her.

The melee had come to a standstill, the man's four guards stubbornly gripping their weapons as the mass of warriors surrounded them.

Jamie Grant's voice boomed over the others, calling out, "Connor, set him down." He emerged from the gates, followed by his brother, Jake, the two of them pushing their way into the middle of the crowd.

Jamie stepped in front of Elizabeth, and Jake did the same with their sire, who promptly pushed him out of the way.

Connor growled, "Fine. I'll set the bastard down." He lowered the alleged accoster until his feet touched down, then promptly plowed his fist into the man's face, sending him crumpling to the ground.

Helped up by his men, he laughed off the attack. "'Twas worth every moment."

Gil had listened to enough. Pushing others aside to get closer to the bastard, he intended to land his own punch for the man's insult to Elizabeth. But her gaze snapped to his, stopping him in his tracks.

He did whatever she wished, especially in front of her father and brothers.

Loki came up behind him and whispered in his ear, "What stopped you? We'd all like to plant a fist in his face."

The words startled Gil, for he'd been careful to hide his feelings, but he concluded Loki thought he was angry for the same reason the rest of them were—because the Englishman was being so boldly crude and disrespectful. Everyone *did* love Elizabeth.

Especially him.

Gil said nothing, afraid to give away his true feelings, instead moving closer to the melee.

Jamie stepped in front of Connor. "You will apologize to my sister, then leave, Baron."

The man's smirk widened.

"Baron Haite, I'll ask you again. Do you have anything to say to my sister?" Jamie asked, his hands on his hips.

The baron, red-faced as a summer apple, turned to face Elizabeth. He motioned for his men to drop their weapons, then paused to catch his breath. "Beth, I enjoyed tasting you. I cannot wait for our marriage." He waggled his brows at her, a huge mistake in Gil's judgment.

Alex grabbed the English fool by the throat and lifted him into the air, setting him down far away from Elizabeth. He whispered one word, "Lads."

Jake, Jamie, and Connor forced the baron's guards back, then Alex unsheathed a dagger. "I will count to ten. If your men have not removed you by then, I will have my sons hold you while I cut your throat, Baron Clifton Haite. And I'd be happy to send your head to King Edward. There'll be no insulting my daughter."

The look on the huge swordsman's face was intimidating enough that Gil felt himself lose color. Even though the man had aged, he and his son, Connor, were still the tallest and most powerful men Gil had ever seen.

"One…two…three…"

The baron nodded and made a motion to his men. He carefully backed away and mounted the horse that had been brought to him. Once he mounted and turned away, he stopped his horse, looking back over his shoulder. "Remember, this match has been approved by King Edward, and he *will* have his way. *We* will have our way. You savage Scots need to learn your place. Beneath us. I'll leave for now, but I will return for my bride." He then cast a snide look at Elizabeth, "Until our wedding day, my dear."

"Never!" Elizabeth shouted. Her balled fists told Gil just how upset she was. The stable lads rushed to bring the Englishmen's horses out, along with a few others, and the useless guards mounted quickly behind their overlord.

Gil said nothing because he didn't wish to upset Elizabeth, but also because he was intimidated by her sire and brothers, two of whom had mounted to escort the baron off Grant land.

But he knew what was in his heart.

He was in love with Elizabeth Grant, and he wouldn't be happy until she was his bride. Six moons. They'd kept their relationship secret for six moons. She'd taken to visiting Castle Curanta to teach the wee bairns who lived with them, and Gil, being only human, had fallen for her. It had come as an utter shock to him to realize she felt the same way. Their situation wasn't conventional, nor would it be accepted, but it worked for them.

Or at least it would until her parents finally grew tired of waiting and forced her to marry someone else.

Alex moved toward his daughter, wrapping his arm around her before he said, "Come, lass. You may talk with your mother and sisters. Did he hurt you in any other way?" He mopped the blood from her lip with a small linen square, a gentle gesture for such a powerful man.

"Nay, Papa. He maneuvered me over to the door quite slyly, then shoved me ahead of him. I'm grateful you heard my shouts. He forced a kiss on me, but I kicked him. I think the nip was for spite, from what little I know of romantic entanglements." Elizabeth looked to her brothers, but they said nothing.

"And pardon me for asking such a ridiculous question, but did you allow him to call you Lizzie or Beth?"

"Nay, Papa. Never."

It was well known on Grant land that Elizabeth had put an end to all the nicknames when she was just over ten years old. Which made it all the more special she'd asked Gil to call her Lizzie.

But someone else using his name for her? He didn't like that thought one bit. Under his breath, Gil swore, "The bastard will never touch you again."

Elizabeth's mother and sisters, Maeve and Kyla, crowded into her chamber. As the youngest lasses, Maeve and Elizabeth used to share a chamber, but Elizabeth had been given her own space years ago, upon turning seven and ten.

"Elizabeth, are you hale?" Kyla asked. "He truly did you no harm?"

Maeve, who was a good deal younger than them, whispered, "Besides biting her lip? 'Tis most painful looking. Men must be animals." At the tender age of two and ten, she had little understanding of relationships just yet.

Her mother patted her shoulder. "Only some men, Maeve. Elizabeth will find herself a fine husband. As you will when your time comes."

"Nay, I'll not marry…ever." Maeve blushed, a color that carried down to her long, graceful neck.

"He did not hurt me," Elizabeth said firmly. "He took me by surprise. I did not expect him to be foolish enough to force himself on me. 'Twas exactly how I described, although he did not steal a kiss so much as push himself against me in a…" She paused, looking at Maeve, then her mother, whose glare convinced her to change the direction of her explanation. "What I mean to say is that I've had men try to steal a kiss before, but never in such a crude way."

Kyla crossed her arms and flounced onto the bed. "You're Alexander Grant's daughter. There isn't a man in all the Highlands who doesn't know better than to treat us as such. We've been well-protected by Papa and by our brothers, too. The baron has a set of bollocks…"

"Kyla!" their mother said a bit too loudly.

"Fine, Mama, but you need to stop coddling Maeve, too," Kyla insisted. "It never hurts to learn about men at a young age. And she needs to know this, too. You should have kneed him right between his legs." Then she turned toward Maeve. "A kick carefully placed to a man's bollocks will stop them immediately. They scream like wee bairns."

Maeve giggled and covered her mouth with her hands. Their mother started to speak, but Kyla held up a hand. "Mama, she needs to know these things. Look at how quickly she's growing."

Maeve was short, with glossy brown hair, and she'd begun to develop curves—her shape very different from Kyla and Elizabeth, who were both tall and willowy. "Have you not noticed how the guards already stare at her?"

"All right, lasses," their mother said in exasperation. "You've explained all to her, but the important question is this. Do you wish to continue with the festival or cancel it, Elizabeth? We can send the other two home if you'd like."

Elizabeth wanted nothing more than to send the other suitors home, but sending them home would hardly put an end to it. If they went home prematurely, they'd have to be invited back, which would offer the kind of encouragement she did not want to give. If someone was invited twice, sent home twice, some sort of explanation would need to be offered. One she couldn't give.

Nay, Mama," she said with a sigh. We've invited everyone, the minstrels are in the great hall, and Cook prepared a feast. There's no reason to allow the baron to ruin it. I'll be happy to converse with the other two who've come for my hand."

So I can get rid of them both. I love Gil.

"Mama, I'll be fine. Give me a few moments alone to prepare myself, and I'll return to the hall. But I'll be remaining inside for the evening."

Her mother came over and wrapped her arms around her. "You have made a wise decision, I think. 'Tis best to carefully consider all of your options. We'll head down and tell your sire you'll be there soon."

Kyla and Maeve each gave her a swift hug before the three left.

Elizabeth let out a long sigh. Sneaking around with Gil was enjoyable—it made her feel alive in a way she savored, and the challenge of pulling such a thing off was equally invigorating—but perhaps she hadn't thought it through.

Someday she and Gil would marry, so why did she want to keep their relationship hidden? Because she enjoyed keeping their love between the two of them. She wasn't ready to have all eyes on them the way they were on her this eve. Everyone watching their every move, the way they gazed into each other's eyes, how often they touched. Being the center of attention, of *speculation*, was not the least bit appealing to her. She wished to love her man and be left alone.

Their arrangement worked for now. Going back and forth between Grant land and Castle Curanta was something she'd done for years, and she loved both places. She also wasn't ready to give up watching over her parents. They were getting on in age, and they needed her. Her mother could no longer handle all the tasks associated with running the keep—calculating meals, ordering fabric, and making sure the clan operated smoothly. Elizabeth had taken over many of her duties, and no one else was aware.

She was needed here. Moving to Castle Curanta was out of the question.

Which meant she and Gil needed to wait until he felt confident enough to move to Grant Castle.

In the meantime, she had to tend to her guests. Enough searching for more reasons to hide her relationship with Gil. They were both happy with the situation, so there was no reason to reveal their secret.

To anyone.

After setting herself to rights in her chamber, Elizabeth came back downstairs to rejoin the festivities in the great hall in Grant Castle. She couldn't stop licking the open sore on her lower lip from the bastard who'd forced himself on her, but she refused to allow him to ruin her night.

The King of England was putting her in a difficult position, offering her hand in marriage in return for a large amount of coin, though her father had insisted they would not honor his choice. She was to make her own choice, a freedom given to all of the Grant children. Still, her parents most definitely had their own thoughts on the subject, and her mama had made no mystery of her preference for their neighbor, Chieftain Symon MacTear. Elizabeth wasn't interested.

Her heart was set on another man, although no one knew. Forbidden love was painful, but she would stay true to her course. The only man she would ever marry was Gil…once she was ready.

Laird MacTear held no more interest for her than the baron, or the other suitor who'd attended to the celebration this eve—a Norseman named Orvar.

When she reached the bottom of the staircase, her sire came to her. He offered his elbow and she took it, sweeping her long skirts away from the staircase as they made their way across the floor. A deep red velvet adorned with gold ribbons on the bodice and at the hems and Grant plaid at the bodice, it had been made specifically for this event.

"You are lovely tonight, daughter," Papa said. "Do not allow that bastard Englishman to tarnish your evening. I'll not allow Edward to force your hand." Her father intentionally referred to Edward without his title, an indication that he supported the Scots' rights to have their own king, something they'd lacked since the untimely death of King Alexander III. The English, of course, had no intention of allowing it.

"My thanks to you for my lovely gown." She tilted her head back to look up at her father, so handsome in his finery. She was taller than most lasses, but she had a long way to go to catch up with her father and brother Connor.

"Did you have a good conversation with your sisters and your mother?"

"I am fine, Papa. You need not worry about me. It takes more than a rude baron to dampen my mood."

"That gown suits you perfectly. It makes your hair seem even more golden," he said with a smile.

Laird MacTear approached them. He looked handsome in his green and gold plaid, the color a pleasant contrast to his dark hair, but he held no interest for Elizabeth. His long hair was tethered in back, the fine strands escaping the tether and floating about his face in a way she found unappealing. He looked much better on his horse with his hair blowing free. Elizabeth was nearly his height, but he had broad shoulders from his sword fighting, something he took pride in.

Her father said, "Did you have a challenge in the lists this morn, MacTear?"

"I always look for a challenge," he said with a smirk, "but seldom find one. You need to train your men harder. My men all make easy work of your guards, Grant. They are turning weak."

Elizabeth had overheard Jamie laughing about Clan MacTear's lack of skills. He thought it entertaining that they bragged about their abilities but could only stand against Clan Grant's newest fighters. The others would embarrass the man, so her father had instructed Jake to make sure they didn't allow the visitors to fight anyone with real talent. The neighbor treaty, her father had called it. There was always much snickering from the observers, and MacTear considered it laughter over the Grant warriors' failures.

Instead, it was the inadequacy of MacTear's men.

As he approached them, he bowed and asked, "May I escort your daughter outside for a short stroll, my lord?"

Elizabeth gave her father's arm a slight squeeze, and he said, "Not at this time, MacTear, but my daughter appreciates your kindness."

Rather than rage as the baron would have done, MacTear simply smiled at Elizabeth and stepped back so they could meander around the large hall, making their way past the revelers seated at the various trestle tables. Members of Clan Grant, of course, but also villagers and visitors.

Her mother approached them, as beautiful as ever, although her hair was more white than blonde now.

"Mama, are you enjoying the festivities?"

Her mother dropped her voice so she could not be overheard. "I would enjoy it more if you would stop this game of squeezing your father's arm every time a man approaches you. You were wise to send the baron away, but there is naught wrong with Laird MacTear. Why did you reject him, Alex?"

"Our daughter had a trying experience earlier. Allow her to stay where she feels safest for a wee bit, Maddie."

"Mama," Elizabeth said, looking into the same blue eyes as her own. "Laird MacTear has been here before. You know I'm not interested in him." She couldn't fault her dear mother for trying. Her parents were the happiest couple she knew, and her mother wanted the same for all of them. Elizabeth found that type of love with Gil, but there was the obstacle of having her parents accept a match with an orphan who lived with Loki Grant. While she didn't truly believe they'd object—others in her family had married outside of their station—she couldn't convince Gil that his lineage wouldn't matter to her parents. He had this whole idea that he had to prove his value to them, raise himself in their eyes to a level above his current situation.

Elizabeth had insisted these thoughts were hogwash—that it was his good heart that mattered, not his ability to wield a sword—but Gil wasn't so easily convinced. He spent hours in the lists with the goal of becoming a swordsman on par with Loki and Connor and Alex Grant. He was convinced that was the only way to prove his worth. So Gil spent his time in the lists while Elizabeth spent her time attempting to waylay her mother's attempts to find a different husband for her. How she wished Maeve were a wee bit older.

The true reason for her mother's persistence was that Elizabeth was well past the marrying age. Perhaps that could work in her favor. Perhaps they'd be grateful she loved Gil.

"Elizabeth," her mother rebuked, "how could you know if he would suit you or not? If you spoke with him just once, you might find you have more in common than you think." She crossed her arms and stared from one to the other. "'Tis time, lass. You can't wait much longer."

"Mama, you worry too much, and I've spoken with him on other visits." She had to admit, Laird MacTear was an acceptable suitor. He was kind and nice-looking, and he didn't live far away. That was important to her, although she'd never said so to anyone. She didn't wish to leave her parents. She had to stay here because...well. If she weren't here, she'd have to rely on others to care for her family—and on her parents to keep her informed. Her trust ran thin in both instances.

Elizabeth had been the youngest for a long time before Maeve was adopted, and she'd been forgotten on more than one occasion. If she ever left home, she was quite certain she'd be the last to learn everything.

"Alex, you must let her go."

"I will when she is ready. I don't treat her any differently than any of our children. I promised my mother my siblings could choose their own mate, and I don't intend to take that right away from my children. What more would you have me do than arrange these festivals to help her find a suitor? When the right one comes along, she'll know."

"Aye, but will you allow it?" her mother asked her father. She wondered if she'd been the source of disagreement between the two. That she didn't want, but the only man who interested her here was Gil.

"Of course, I would, my dear," Papa said, leaning down to kiss her mother's cheek.

No one was surprised that Alex Grant coddled his youngest daughter. He'd said from the day Madeline Grant carried their first-born that he wished to have a golden-haired lassie with blue eyes like Maddie. First had come the twin lads, dark-haired Jake and fair-haired Jamie, then Kyla with dark hair and blue eyes of her mother. Then Connor, dark-haired with gray eyes, a look-alike to his father.

So it was only fitting that the last child born to them had been the blonde-haired girl with blue eyes. She'd settled on his lap when she was young, and it had quickly become her favorite place to be in the world. As a wee bairn, she'd never wanted to be far from her sire.

Not much had changed. Oh, they'd adopted Maeve when Elizabeth was two and ten, but Elizabeth had never felt threatened. Her parents had big enough hearts to love both of them and she'd been excited to have a new sister.

She wasn't ready to leave, even though part of her heart was now with Gil. Even though she was three and twenty, past the normal age of marrying, they'd marry someday, but it didn't need to be anytime soon. She liked things just the way they were.

Little did she know how that was all about to change.

CHAPTER TWO

GIL NEVER MOVED far from the table that held all the food. After spending part of his life as an orphan, which meant forever going hungry, the scents of food had always had the power to draw him in. Elizabeth had been in charge of setting the menu, and she'd done a fine job working with the beloved cook of Grant Castle. It was also the one spot where he could see everything that took place in the great hall.

When he reflected on his life, the most difficult part had been the years he'd spent alone and hungry. Add to that the fear of cruel men in a castle who liked to hit with their fists, and Gil had many reasons to be grateful that horrific period in his life was behind him. But more than anything, he appreciated the connection he'd formed with Lizzie, and thus would never risk losing her. Holding back during the previous situation had stretched his limits of control, but he'd survived, only because the men who protected her on Grant land were the fiercest in all of Scotland.

His gaze often followed Lizzie, but he also made it a point to notice other lasses, just so his friends did not catch on. He glanced at Brodie's two daughters, Catriona and Alison, and Maeve, all beautiful in different ways.

Unfortunately, his gaze also stayed on Alex Grant, fearful the great man would someday see the want in Gil's eyes. The day he realized who Gil wanted, Alex would ban him from Grant land, never to be seen again, *if* he allowed him to live. He also had to be wary of all three of Elizabeth's brothers, though Connor was the most likely to catch on. Elizabeth had told him she was closest to Connor, who was the youngest of the three and had paid her more attention after Jamie and Jake were made co-lairds. She'd also been close with Kyla, but their relationship had changed when Kyla started having bairns of her own, something that tied her up more than Elizabeth would have liked. She felt forgotten by her elder sister. And her younger sister, while sweet, was too young for the two to confide in each other.

While Lizzie often felt forgotten and neglected, he didn't believe it to be true.

Gil didn't agree—he saw the way Kyla kept a protective eye on her sister—and he also thought she was his biggest chance of meeting the Grants' approval as a suitor. After all, he'd helped Finlay save Kyla from an enemy castle many years ago.

Gil felt the need to prove himself, especially to Alexander Grant. He worked hard to prepare for the day when he would need to show himself to be a worthy suitor, but he didn't think Lizzie was ready for that yet. She worried about leaving her parents, and Gil was dedicated to Loki and the orphans of Castle Curanta. The only place he dared venture was to Grant Castle. He never went elsewhere.

Never.

Loki sidled up next to him. "When will you take action on your choice?"

"What?" Gil asked, astounded by his question. Loki, who'd welcomed him into his home, who'd introduced him to the boys who had become his closest friends. His brothers. He was especially close to Kenzie, but Thorn and Nari, who'd joined their group several years back, were both good lads, and he was forever loyal to them too. Neither he nor Kenzie had married yet, instead devoting themselves to helping Loki wherever they were needed. Thorn and Nari were still young, Thorn at five and ten while Nari was a year younger, but they'd grown quickly and worked hard in the lists to be allowed to travel with the warriors on patrols.

It was as if they had an unspoken bond that none of the four of them would ever leave. They were the orphans, the lads, and they stayed together.

"I think your gaze is on someone, but I haven't quite determined whom. Are you smitten, lad? But why hide it? There are many lovely lassies here, so no one would blame you for marrying. If you've found someone on Grant land, say the word. I'll speak with Alex on your behalf."

"Nay, you have it wrong," he insisted. "I'm not interested in anyone. I have too much to do at Castle Curanta, Chief."

Loki clasped his shoulder. "Do as you wish and keep it private for now, but you lads need to find someone. Each of you. Don't let your time waste away before 'tis too late for you to have your own son or daughter. They'll all enrich your life more than you could imagine.

"I'll keep that in mind, Chief."

Jake called out to Loki, so he quickly moved away, much to Gil's relief. He let out the breath he was holding, pleased to be alone again so his glance could once more stray to Elizabeth. She looked simply stunning, although she stayed close to her sire at all times. He watched as she sent Laird MacTear on his way, and the man did not look happy.

Would he retaliate the same way the baron had?

He didn't think so, if only because the man's land was so close to Grant land. He probably depended on the Grants for protection. His army of guards was paltry compared to the number training in the Grant lists.

Elizabeth swept her skirts in a wide arc as she headed toward the kitchens, probably to make certain Cook had prepared enough for the feast. He knew she'd assumed many duties for maintaining the keep after Kyla started having bairns. Maddie gave instructions, but it was mostly up to Elizabeth to see that their many needs were met.

And she did a fine job.

He was surprised when Maeve came up to him a few moments later and whispered in his ear. "My sister requests your assistance in the cellar. She needs to bring up another cask of ale, and I cannot assist her."

"I'll help her," he said, moving toward the kitchens. The thought of going down into the cellars made him shudder, but he couldn't deny her, not even in this.

Ever since his days in service of Simon de La Porte and Glenn Buchan, the cruel men who'd kidnapped Kyla, he'd had a severe hatred of cellars. That was where he'd stayed in Buchan Castle—

the foul dungeons. Dirty, gloomy, damp, and repulsive. The smells weren't what had repelled him so much as his fear of the mighty fists of de La Porte. The man could swing his huge paw and catch one completely unaware. It was a wonder he hadn't lost an eye to the man's bullying tactics.

Kyla could have easily done so, as de La Porte had beaten her as if she were the lowliest man in the castle. How it had pained Gil to see him treat a woman so. But Kyla and Finlay had come out of the situation safely, and the men who'd tormented them were, rightfully, dead for their trespasses against Clan Grant.

Still…

The cellars had a way of bringing the old memories back in a wild fury.

But he'd not miss this chance to be alone with Elizabeth. He stepped into the kitchens and made his way around the periphery, ignoring all the busy servants and cooks, just as they ignored him. Once at the back, he opened the door to the cellars and closed it behind him, relying on the one torch at the base to lead him through the maze.

Pleased to see the Grants kept their cellars much cleaner than Buchan, he headed down the passageway, taking a deep breath to help banish the memories and focus on the prospect of seeing the woman he loved.

A hand came out of a chamber and grabbed him by the elbow. He nearly swung out but stayed his hand because the hand that reached for him was quite dainty, and the scent attached to it was one he recognized.

Elizabeth tugged him close, and he wrapped his arms around her and kissed her, pulling back slightly to make sure she was accepting of his ravishment.

"Aye, more, Gil."

He needed no more encouragement than the sly smile he saw by the flame of the distant torch. He kissed her, plundering her delicious mouth until she backed up against the cold stone wall. The only thing that could stop him was the taste of the blood on her lip. Remembering what the baron had done, he pulled away and reached up to gently touch the wound there. "I'm hurting you where the bastard drew blood."

Her fingers threaded through his thick, dark hair, and she pulled him close again. "You could never hurt me. Kiss me again."

He couldn't deny her, his lips meeting hers, though he made a point of being a bit more tender, of reining in his base instincts to ravage her and lift her up so he could thrust inside her.

He kissed a trail down her neck and across the delicate bone beneath it, dropping to the cleavage hidden behind a small piece of fabric. Elizabeth reached for a tie, undoing it, and deftly lifted one breast out for his ravishment. He growled as he lifted the soft mound and took her nipple in his mouth, suckling her until she cried out and arched against him. He grazed his teeth over the taut peak and she whimpered, collapsing against him.

"Do it, Gil. I need you inside me. We have time."

Her words stopped him but not because they'd never been intimate. Although he knew it was wrong, although he knew Alex would flay him if he knew the truth, they had already experienced that joy. Many, many times.

"Here? With your sire just above us? He'd hang my head on a pike if he caught us." He took a step back, doing his best to fix her gaping bodice, then returned his hands to her hips. "You are out of your mind, lass. I want you, but not like this. 'Tis too dangerous."

Bold as she was, she reached for him beneath his plaid, gripping him with the skill he knew she had, moving her hand in a way that nearly had him moaning, but he stilled her movement. "Please, Lizzie. I cannot take it."

"I was hoping you could not," she said with a smirk.

His breathing had reached a feverish pitch, but he refused to do as she asked. The dark shadows behind her and a sudden sound from above froze both of them. "I would love naught more, but I cannot, Lizzie. The cellars remind me of the dungeons in Buchan Castle. You know what that does to me…" His words caught in his throat as the memories assaulted him.

His breathing returned to normal as the dark thoughts dampened his arousal. "Lizzie," he whispered, setting his forehead against hers while he took both of her hands. "Please, no more torment. We'll find another way, but not down here." He closed his eyes to take in her scent, the feel of the silky strands of her hair, usually plaited, tempting him more than he'd care to admit. Lizzie had a way of keeping him grounded, of banishing the evil thoughts away.

How he wished he could forget them entirely.

She brought her hands up to cup his face. "Forgive me, Gil. It didn't occur to me. Meet me near the back wall an hour after all have left. We'll go to our favorite spot."

"Aye, I'd like that."

He held her close, tucking her head beneath his chin and thanking the Lord that this woman loved him.

He didn't know how he'd ever become so fortunate, and he prayed he'd never lose her.

A sudden uncanny inkling climbed up the back of his neck, much like a cold serpent, but he shook it off.

"Come. I'll escort you up the staircase."

As they walked away, he couldn't help but look back over his shoulder to see if something had indeed fallen.

Of course, there was no snake.

Elizabeth made Gil leave the cellars the other way, through an exit leading directly outside. She didn't think it wise to be caught in the cellars with him. She made her way up, stopped to talk to the cook about needing more spices when they went to market, then stepped back into the great hall.

She was instantly surrounded by three lads wielding swords—her wee nephews. Oh, how she loved them.

Alasdair said, "We're here to protect you from the baron or any other suitors who don't treat you right. We heard he tried to attack you, Aunt Elizabeth."

"We'll fight them off," Alick said.

Els nodded furiously. "Aye, they'll not get past us."

The three lads had been born on the same night, the firstborn grandsons of Alexander Grant, only none could claim that honor because according to Aunt Jennie and Aunt Brenna they had been born at the same exact time, thus putting an end to the rivalry among their parents, all of whom had wanted their lad to be the first.

"Lads, my thanks, but I don't think I'll be needing you this eve."

Now six winters, they grew more endearing each year, Alasdair dark-haired, Alick flame-haired, and Els fair.

"Just the same, we'll stay." Alasdair searched the hall for any strangers who might harass her.

A tow-haired lass much shorter than the three sauntered up and said to the boys, "You are fools. Aunt Elizabeth could take them all out with her slinger. She does not need your help. Lasses can take care of themselves." Dyna, her wee niece, was a year and a half younger than the lads, but they always seemed to do as she suggested. No one could figure out why the lass had such control over them, but they let it be.

A serving lass passed them with a heaping platter, and Alick took one look at it and started moving. "Here come the fruit pies. I'm getting two now." He disappeared as quickly as a firefly.

"Not before I do," Els shouted behind him.

Alasdair managed to shove between the two and grab the first fruit pie as soon as the platter was set on the table, a smug grin on his face.

The lads continued their bickering as they ate the steaming pies, but Elizabeth's attention was fixed on Dyna. She had to have a word with the wee one. "How did you know?" she asked. "I've never used it on Grant land. Only at Castle Curanta." She'd learned from Gil. To her knowledge, no one had ever witnessed their lessons, especially no one from Grant land.

Dyna lifted her chin and pointed to Elizabeth's side. "'Tis in your pocket, is it not?" She gave her an unnervingly direct look. Wee Dyna could be very sweet, but she was different. Something about her was very different, indeed.

Some believed she was a seer.

Elizabeth hoped not, because if she was, she would surely know about Gil.

Reaching into her pocket, she felt for the small weapon, relieved to find it was still there. It hadn't been hanging out of her pocket though, which eliminated the only easy explanation for why Dyna had guessed it was there. "How did you know?"

Dyna shrugged and walked away, tossing her plait over her shoulder as she spoke. "The same way I know your other secrets."

Rather than ask what secrets she spoke of, Elizabeth settled for a more honest approach. "Remember, they're meant to stay secrets."

Dyna nodded as she made her way through the crowd.

No one would listen to the gossip of a four-year-old, would they?

CHAPTER THREE

LATER THAT NIGHT, after most of the crowd had departed, Elizabeth made her way through the kitchens, grabbing the old brown mantle she kept hidden in the back, a cast off from the serving lasses that she'd kept for herself. It wasn't a normal color for her—she preferred blue, which brought out her eyes—so no one would ever suspect it was her under the faded hood. This was part of her charade, the only way to sneak outside the gates. She'd prepared carefully for this event over the last several weeks, putting all the steps in place—the old mantle, the key to the back door in the curtain wall, the best place for her to hide her sweet mare in the woods.

First she'd feigned exhaustion and gone to her chamber, then she'd changed her clothing, carefully folding the beautiful gown she'd worn in favor of a gown that was old and unbecoming. She'd waited until the noise in the great hall diminished to a light buzz, then made her way down the stairs, to the back exit, out of the keep. All was carefully planned, just as it always was whenever Gil was on Grant land. She'd not be waylaid.

It didn't matter how she looked as long as she could be in the arms of her lover.

Sadly, she arrived before Gil, but that wasn't unusual. He made a point of doing everything carefully, to guarantee he would get away without being seen. The men liked to drink and chat about the latest events, and the baron had given them plenty to talk about this eve. It would take some conniving on his part not to be missed.

She wrapped her arms around her horse, Midnight Sun, cuddling her. The sweet-natured mare would help Elizabeth stay warm while she waited.

She didn't have to wait long. Midnight Sun gave a wee whinny to signal someone else had emerged from the back gate, but she didn't move until she knew for sure the person was Gil. She held her arms out for him, and he swept her in a warm embrace, shoving her hood back and her scarf aside to nuzzle her neck, something she loved.

A warm tongue teased her earlobe, and she squealed, as quietly as she could. He knew how she loved that quick tease.

And so did her horse. Midnight Sun nudged them with her muzzle, nickering, as if she wished to be involved. Elizabeth pushed on the beast's neck and stepped out from under her. "Shameless, Sunny. You are such a flirt. You are quite jealous of this handsome man standing in front of me, are you not? You wish for his attention to be just on you." She kissed Gil's neck, then pulled back.

"Enough teasing," he growled, tossing her up onto the horse and climbing up behind her effortlessly. He took the reins and headed Midnight Sun down the path they'd made wider for their trysts.

Gil would do anything to make Lizzie happy. Even sneak around behind her sire's back, risking his life. While she knew her father wouldn't kill him, he had to be a wee bit nervous about dallying with the daughter of such a renowned swordsman.

"Lizzie, you are set to tease me this eve, and I know not how much I can handle," he whispered, his warm breath tickling the side of her face.

"We have been separated for too long this time."

"Say the word, and I'll offer for you. I cannot stand watching you with another man. When I arrived on Grant land and saw the melee, I could hardly control my anger. Had your brothers and father not been taking care of that arrogant bastard, I would have stepped in. 'Tis a difficult position to be in, Lizzie. We should marry. I doubt your sire would accept me, but we have to try."

He said nothing, awaiting her answer, but they'd discussed this before and always came to the same conclusion. Neither of them was ready to leave home or upset their lives just yet. It would affect too many people.

There was a long pause before she spoke, but he didn't rush her. "I do believe my sire will accept you with my encouragement, but I don't think they're ready for me to leave them yet. And you're not prepared to leave Castle Curanta. Sabina would be devastated."

Sabina was one of the young orphans who lived at Castle Curanta. She'd arrived at the same time their relationship started, and working with the wee lass was something they did together. Devastated by her parents' deaths, she'd been found wandering the streets of Ayr as a toddler, sobbing and filthy. The nun who'd found her had brought her straight to the kirk, feeding her and cleaning her as best they could.

"I know. Before we left for this trip, I had to sit down, cuddle her, and promise her I'd be back and bring you with me shortly after." He leaned into her, pulling her hood down and nuzzling her neck.

Even that small touch shot through her like a flame, torching her insides with need for him. No matter how often they were together, that flame never dimmed. "She's so attached to you, Gil. She needs consistency in her life, and that's what you are for her."

"Aye, but we will be a part of Sabina's life wherever we live. We need only show her that. There's someone else I must prove myself to."

"Loki knows your value, Gil. Kenzie is his second, but you're always there for him."

"'Tis not Loki I need to impress, lass, and you know it."

How she wished he could see his own worth, something that was so clear to her. "Papa and my brothers know what a strong warrior you are. They trust you and respect you. You need to get past your need to impress my family. When the time comes, you'll be accepted, but we should wait a wee bit longer. Give Sabina some time to adjust, and my mother and father more time to prepare for losing me."

"I think they're ready, lass," he said in a soft voice. "Wasn't this festival held so you might find a husband?"

Lizzie chose to ignore his remark, although she knew he was probably right. Her parents *could* lose her now, and her mother had made it very clear she thought the time had come for her to marry. Gil knew as well as she did that *she* was the one who wasn't ready.

"You need to forget impressing my sire," she said.

"Do not say so because the opportunity may have finally arrived," Gil said, giving her temple a quick kiss. "Kenzie is having some issues with his knee, so he may not be able to travel with him for a while. 'Tis the exact opportunity I've been looking for. I can prove myself and then ask for your hand." He tugged on the reins now that they'd moved away from the castle wall, giving the horse her freedom to gallop as she wished, something Elizabeth loved to see.

She nodded to him. "But not much longer, Gil. I fear my mother has convinced herself I should marry Symon MacTear."

"Your sire won't force you to marry against your will. You have him wrapped around every one of your fingers. 'Tis true."

"Your reasoning is true except for one small point."

"What?" he asked, tucking her closer.

"My sire will do anything my mother asks of him too, and if I cannot convince my mother that MacTear is a bad match, she will bend my father's will to hers."

"You must convince her to wait. A year, no more. If I manage to prove my worth, convince Sabina she's in a safe place, and win acceptance from your father, your sisters, and brothers..."

"Enough!" she chided. "I do not need to be reminded of the obstacles facing us. You have to be willing to move to Grant land first."

"What about six moons here and six moons at Castle Curanta?" He nuzzled her a little more, nipping her neck playfully.

She could almost see his grin. Gil had always been a negotiator. It was one of the reasons she loved him so. Fortunately, the small hut hidden in the woods came in view. Midnight Sun knew it well and knickered as if to say she was glad they'd finally arrived.

"Sunny," Elizabeth said, "you are just hoping for apples. We'll see if the apple tree has any fruit left." Most likely not, given it was early winter, but the beast was forever hopeful. If she could find her way into the hut, she'd eat all the apples they'd stored in a basket for winter.

Once they arrived, Gil hopped off the large horse and lifted her down, stopping to kiss her quickly.

"Inside," she scolded. "'Tis too cool out here for me. I wish to be not far from the fire you're about to build." She knew Gil always made sure there was plenty of firewood near the hearth before they left.

They had found this place last spring, when their relationship had progressed to an intimacy level that required more privacy and comfort than the grass under the pine trees had given them. Even though she'd encouraged him to finish the deed under the stars, Gil would not have it, swearing he would only risk such a thing if they were somewhere they could not be seen. Then, as if guided by some benevolent magic, they'd found this deserted hut. Gil had fixed the broken boards and the leaking thatch overhead, while Elizabeth had made a new mattress stuffed with heather and covered it with thick furs and warm plaids she'd smuggled in from the castle. She'd brought fresh rushes and found a small table with two small chairs, which had worked well enough until Gil finished building a chair large enough for the both of them. They set it directly in front of the hearth, where they spent much of their time together.

Once inside, Gil moved to the hearth and started a fire while Elizabeth removed her mantle, set a bottle of wine along with a hunk of cheese on the table, and arranged the bed just to her liking.

Then she moved over to marvel at the chair he'd made, running her finger along the smooth surface of the arm. They had the best conversations in that chair. Elizabeth had made a thick cushion, and the place felt like it was their home. How she adored that feeling. "Gil, I love being at your cottage, but this place is even more special. It feels as though 'tis our verra own, that we're married and living here together. Whenever we're here, I never wish to leave." Gil, Kenzie, Thorn, and Nari each had their own cottages in the small village outside Castle Curanta, though Thorn and Nari spent more time together than apart. His, thankfully, was far from the gates and private enough for them to be alone together. A talented woodworker, he'd made his place beautiful, full of detailed and finely made furniture. "You could sell many chairs like this one, just because it's so large."

"My sire taught me well. He made the best cloth to smooth the wood just so, and I always enjoyed helping him with the sanding." He sat back on his heels, staring off into space. "'Tis one of my fondest memories of my sire. Fishing and woodworking. He was a quiet man, but he showed us he cared through his work. I still remember the chest he made for my mother. The drawers were so perfectly fitted, they barely made a sound."

"'Tis too bad you didn't get to keep any of the pieces your father made."

"I have no idea who lives in our old cottage now. I was pushed out by some men who were much bigger than me."

"Oh, Gil," she said, moving over to his side and massaging his neck while he worked on the fire. "How you question your strength is beyond my comprehension. My brothers never had to find their way alone, hunt for all their food." She peered at him from behind, admiring the muscles in his neck and his shoulders as he worked. "Nor did they have to bury their own sire. I could hold you in my arms forever simply because of that one fact." A spark caught in the brush and spread the fire through the logs.

As soon as she heard the crackle of the flames, she squealed and jumped to her feet to do her favorite dance.

How she loved to tease Gil. He stood and spun around as soon as he heard her loosening the ties on her bodice. Removing her clothes as slowly as possible, she stepped over next to the fire, then freed her breasts from their confinement, giggling at the tautness of her nipples.

"'Twas looking at me that caused that, not the cold," Gil said, puffing his chest out as if he truly believed what he'd just said.

"Of course it was," she said coyly, going along with his tale. She stepped in front of him and gave him her back. "I do need help with the ties, please."

"Gladly," he said, kissing the flesh beneath each of the ties as he undid them. When he reached the curve of her firm bottom, he slid his hands into the opening of her gown and slid it off. "You are cold, my sweet. Should I warm you back here or do you need it more across your chest?"

She shimmied around in a wide circle, taking him with her

until her breasts faced the dancing flames. Glancing over her shoulder, she whispered, "My bottom does indeed need the heat of your soft caress."

He did as she asked, and she closed her eyes to the delightful torture as his hands kneaded her backside, a part of her that was incredibly sensitive. As he continued his ministrations, his hands caressing over her hips to the front, dipping in her slick folds, he brought her close, just where she needed him.

She reached over her shoulder and deftly unclasped his brooch, dropping his plaid to the ground. Whirling around as fast as she could, she yanked his tunic up and over his head, leaving him in nothing but his wool hose and his boots.

She let out a wee whistle as she leaned into him, running her fingers between his dark chest hairs before moving down to grasp him fully in her hand. "You are a fine specimen of a man, Gil Grant."

All he could do was give a moan. He helped her remove the rest of her clothing, then lifted her into his arms so quickly she squealed and he tossed her onto the bed, settling down beside her. "My lady, are you ready for this?"

"I surely am, my lord," she said, spreading her legs for him.

"Lizzie, my sweet Lizzie, have you any idea how much I have missed you? We are too far apart sometimes," he said, kissing a path down her jawline, nibbling on her ear, then down her neck, across her chest until he took her nipple in her mouth and suckled her, causing her to cry out and buck against him. "Easy, lass. We have plenty of time, no reason to rush this."

"Gil, I need you now. I thought about you all last eve in my bed. I awakened in the middle of the night, drenched in sweat. I reached for you but you were not there. I was left alone and wanting you."

He chuckled. "And did you touch yourself then?"

"Nay," she said, playfully slapping his shoulder as he kissed down the middle of her chest, beneath her breasts and down her belly. "I wanted you. That would not have been enough for me. And I want you now even more."

"Oh, you'll have me, lass," he said, lifting his head and peering up at her. "First my tongue and then the rest of me. Because of last night, I suspect you're already close to going over the edge, so I'll make sure you get there quickly. Otherwise you'll finish before I thrust inside you twice."

"Oh, Gil…" She grabbed his thick hair with one hand but didn't yank like she wanted to, instead running her hands through his strands as he did just as he'd promised. He kissed her there, in that spot that rendered her speechless.

He parted her curls and teased her everywhere with his tongue, sucking and laving until she screamed his name out, falling into her release with a surrender that went on and on. "Oh, Gil…"

She cupped his face as he kissed his way back up her body, leaning on his elbow and using his fingers to continue his onslaught of every sensitive spot on her body. Luxuriating in the remnants of her pleasure, she grabbed his arm and stared at him, whispering, "I love you so. We belong together forever."

"Aye, we do. Someday we won't have to part anymore, but in the meantime, we have this." His fingertips grazed the inside of each thigh, then up her belly to tease each breast, his fingers expertly caressing each mound before lightly squeezing her nipples. "Let me know when you're ready for more, Lizzie."

She whimpered as his hand dropped to the vee between her legs again. "Do you need more teasing?" He knew exactly where to touch her and how to make her thrash about like a strumpet. Leaning back and closing her eyes, she gave in to the pleasure he brought her, knowing he would want her to climax again. For some odd reason, whenever she finished, he did the same right after she did.

"Nay," she said, her need for him growing inside her again until it became a powerful need, the kind that made her want him to thrust into her hard, be punishing in his pursuit of both of their pleasures. "Nay," she said, her voice more demanding. "Now. I need you now. Enough teasing."

He settled himself above her, and she wrapped her hand around his hardness, arranging him exactly where she wanted him, but he pushed her hand away, "Nay, 'tis my turn, lassie. You tell me if I'm too rough or if I do anything you don't like?"

"Of course I would, but I know you'd never hurt me. Take me now. Please, Gil." She spread her legs wider, lifting her pelvis for him.

He pushed against her entrance, and she trembled in anticipation. "More."

Instead, he pulled back. "Are you sure you're ready? I want to watch you come again."

"Aye."

Teasing her entrance again, he thrust in a little deeper before pulling back out, his breathing deep and ragged. She loved to hear that sound from him, knowing it was all for her. She raked her finger across one of his nipples, and he growled, pushing into her again. Not wanting him to pull out, to tease, she grabbed his other nipple, squeezing the hard pebble until he groaned and plunged into her, finally giving in to his need.

She moaned with relief as he filled her, stalling just for an instant while he gathered his control again. Then he gave in to the passion, driving into her with a force that made her gasp. Shifting just a bit so his strokes would hit the place she needed them to, she grinned as he grasped her legs and found exactly the right spot. She leveraged her legs to match his rhythm until she shattered again, her release coming hard, being wonderfully vocal because she knew he liked it. Her moans brought him with her as he stiffened, and they convulsed together, their bodies entwined in a mix of sweat and pleasure.

Neither of them spoke in the quiet after the storm. Gil rolled to her side, wrapping both of his arms around her and kissing her forehead, his ragged breathing matching her own. "Do you know how beautiful you are when you find your release? I wish I had the ability to hold my own so I could just watch every part of you."

She melded every part of her body to his, taking in his heat, still awed by the wonder of their lovemaking, how each and every time was so wonderfully different. So beautifully the same. The scent of their union filled the air, and she kissed his shoulder and his neck.

"Be careful what you play with, lass."

"I'll stop," she said. "But I came twice and you only did once."

"Mine was so good it was worth two. Besides, once I fill you with wine and bread, mayhap we'll go again."

After they finished their sweet lovemaking, Gil wrapped them each in a plaid, then lifted Lizzie and moved to the chair in front of the hearth, the wine and cheese from her saddlebags arranged next to them on the table. He offered her a sip of wine from the one goblet they shared. "'Tis a fine bottle you found," he commented.

"We have many more in the cellar."

"Does no one miss the ones you take?" he asked, swallowing a large gulp of the smooth red liquid.

"Nay, because there are so many of us who favor wine. I've even caught Gracie sneaking a bottle to her chamber, and Kyla drinks more of it than I do." She sat sideways on his lap, her legs bent at the knees over the arm of the chair. She loved to kick them about when they were together. The lack of clothing on them felt quite freeing, or so she always told him.

"Lass, what are we doing? Why do we hide? When we get caught..." He'd admitted before, more than once, that he was haunted by the thought of someone in a Grant plaid knocking on the door of this cottage, interrupting them. He knew it would stain his honor forever, even if her father allowed them to marry.

"*If* we get caught..."

"All right. If we ever get caught, I will be so ashamed that I will die of embarrassment. I'll be sent to move boulders from one end of the keep to the other. All by myself. And I'll deserve it. I cannot bear to think of anyone finding out. It could be any of your brothers, your sire, your sisters. Or Magnus, Loki, Finlay, I think I feel ill..."

She placed her two fingers over his lips. "Stop, Gil. Do you seriously think all of my relatives waited until they were married to have relations?" She cut a hunk of cheese off with the dagger and fed it to him, his lips kissing the tip of her finger.

"Honestly, 'tis not something I've thought of before. You wish to tell tales on your relatives? I'll listen." If she told him a believable story, perhaps the sweat on his brow would cease.

"I've heard them talking before. I don't know about my parents, but my uncle Robbie said he had relations with Aunt Caralyn in the abbey. *In the abbey!*" She giggled over that revelation, something she found oddly erotic, an image of herself wearing a nun's habit overtaking her. She threw her head back, overcome with laughter. "Me in a nun's robes and you in a priest's collar. Could you imagine?" She couldn't help but glance over her shoulder, as if afraid someone was listening to her crude talk.

"Could you do it?" she whispered into his ear.

"I'm not sure I could. 'Tis a bit surprising. And blasphemous, do you not think? What about your brothers?"

She thought for a moment. "Jamie and Gracie were forced to marry because some fool man tried to steal her away and marry her, so they may not have had relations. Connor and Sela? Aye, they did before. In fact, they had relations in the abbey too. Sela teased him about it. He visited her there a few times before they married. That leaves Jake. Hmmm...Jake has always been more private about everything. He didn't even tell anyone Aline was carrying before she had Alasdair. He hasn't said anything, but I've heard others whisper. And they're not the only ones. Ashlyn and Magnus were snowed in together for a week before they married, and everyone knows they didn't just sit talking. And my cousin Lily talks about laying with Kyle in a cave. He was afraid to touch her with the wolves watching."

She laughed at that, kicking her legs.

"Why does that strike you so?"

"I love Lily. She's carefree, and the twins are just like her. I don't know how Kyle has survived the three of them. They just had a wee laddie, and Kyle takes him everywhere Papa said." She rested her chin on her hand. "I have the best relatives, Gil. I'm sorry you never knew yours."

"I'm quite pleased to be a member of Clan Grant, and I have plenty of family members at Castle Curanta. I consider Kenzie, Thorn, and Nari my brothers."

"Aye, you do have a wonderful group. 'Tis why you don't wish to leave them..." She tipped her head at him and pursed her lips.

He arched a brow at her. "Just as you're not ready to leave your parents. Soon, though."

"I'll need more of Bella's concoction. I don't wish to be with child before I marry, or my sire will have my head." She rubbed her hand in a circular motion around the large muscle in his upper arm, something she found oddly soothing.

"I don't think you would need to worry about your head. It may be a different part of my body that would be at risk." He gave her a lopsided grin, and she shrugged her shoulders.

"I suppose you could be correct in that assessment. We are risking much."

"You didn't say anything earlier. Do you agree that we should approach your sire within the year? I think Sabina will be fine by then."

She nodded, hoping that she would indeed be ready. She loved the sound of it, yet she hesitated. It all seemed right until she actually made the move to speak to her parents, then her tongue thickened to the size of a loaf of coarse dark bread, as if it would choke her should she speak the words.

He studied her. "When we do this, Lizzie, we both need to make the choice to devote ourselves to our marriage. If I move here to be with you, I'll need you to step back from your clan a wee bit, too. We have to do this together."

She kissed his cheek because it was easier than arguing with him. But she had to admit he was right. Until she was ready, nothing would change.

CHAPTER FOUR

GIL SAT AT the trestle table the next morning with Loki and his group, everyone awaiting Elizabeth's arrival. The visiting laird and the Norseman Orvar had refused to sit down and eat until she arrived, although everyone else had taken a seat. Gil's table laughed and joked among all the others who had crowded into the great hall. They didn't often eat extravagant meals in the morn, but many had shown up just because everyone knew Alex and Maddie would have as much food today as they did last eve.

Orvar was tall and fair-haired, his head a mass of waves that always appeared as if they were in need of a comb. He stood as regal as any king, with the insulting habit of staring down his nose at everyone but Elizabeth. Although his gaze did soften whenever he looked at her, Gil would wager the only person Orvar loved was himself. The man's second, Sten, had hair as straight as a stick. Shorter than Orvar, he looked more powerful because he spent most of his time flexing his muscles. His flaring nostrils gave his emotions away before he ever opened his mouth to speak.

A sudden hush fell over the hall, and he knew it was her before he looked up. She came across the balcony with a whoosh, her skirts rustling around her. Down the stairs she came, her head held high like the most regal of queens, wearing a rose-colored gown that emphasized all her curves, something that Gil had a difficult time handling. She took the hand of the first man at the base of the staircase, Orvar, as she tipped her head to him.

Orvar escorted her to the dais, the one where her parents sat with the two lairds and their wives. Every man's gaze followed her, and Gil had to pull his away, clearing his throat in an attempt to banish the awful taste in his mouth. If her admirers could have drooled without being embarrassed, they would have. He glanced at Nari, who stared openly at Elizabeth, the desire in his eyes unmistakable. "Truly, Nari? You want her that badly?" he drawled, not surprised to see Nari's eyes widen at his declaration.

Nari earned an elbow from Thorn and a shocked look from Loki. The lad blushed, something warriors were not supposed to do.

"Good morn to you, Mama and Papa," Lizzie said, leaning down to kiss her father's cheek. "How do you fare on this cheery morn?"

Her smile was enough to make any morn cheery. Clearly he wasn't the only one who thought so, for Laird MacTear hustled over and shoved Orvar to the side, grabbing Elizabeth's elbow before she could evade him.

The two were about to battle over the lass he loved as if she were fresh meat. This was about to be the greatest test of his control. He'd prefer to put a fist in both of their faces rather than sit and watch this ridiculous contest of wills and arrogance.

"Greetings, Laird MacTear," she said with a brief nod, though Gil could see she was a bit annoyed by the way he'd rudely barged in.

Gil had to get out of his chair and go for another drink just so he could keep an eye on Elizabeth without appearing to do so.

"Good morn to you, my lady. You look lovely as always." The laird gave her what appeared to be a sincere smile, but Gil felt himself bristling.

He needed to keep his hands away from the man.

Elizabeth's three nephews flew down the stairs with their small wooden swords in hand. Alasdair pushed directly in front of the Norseman, but the man's second, the burly oaf called Sten, picked him up and set him behind them. The lad did not like that, as evidenced by Alasdair's sword swinging down in a wide arc, the wood smacking Sten's hand with a loud sound.

"You wee wild thing, stop with the sword." He took the sword from Alasdair and broke it over his knee. Then he tried to strike Alasdair, but the boy was too quick.

That brought Els and Alick to his defense, swinging wildly

while Alasdair launched at the man with his fists. "You'll not hurt any of us, especially Aunt Elizabeth."

The voices reached a loud din but Alex put an end to it, standing from his seat and bellowing, "Lads!" Jamie came out and grabbed Els, while Jake grabbed Alasdair and Alick.

Once they stopped, Sten brushed his hands in front of them with a smirk.

Alex turned to him, his expression flat. "You'll take your leave, Sten."

"What? Why?" he asked, his face turning a bright red.

"You broke one of my grandson's possessions and tried to hit him. You'll leave the hall and not come back."

Gil noticed Alasdair looked as if he were about to break into tears. He buried his face in his sire's waist, mumbling, "Grandpapa gave me that sword."

Glad that his attention didn't stand out amidst the growing crowd, he continued to watch the events as they happened in front of him. It was as if the minstrels had planned the show for them this morn.

The great hall was quite full at the moment, but in between bouts of words, it was so silent they would have all heard a feather fall to the floor. Gil did his best not to smile at the lads, but how he admired them for not being afraid of the daft men in front of them.

Orvar nodded to the man, and Sten left, his feet stomping all the way across the floor. Once the door shut behind him, Orvar turned to Alex. "My apologies to the lads and to you, Laird Grant." Even though he was no longer laird, many gave him the respect by using the title.

Jake sent the three lads back up the stairs. "We'll get you another sword later, lad," he called after them.

Alasdair ran ahead of the other two, his shoulders shaking as if the tears had finally shaken loose.

Laird MacTear said, "Do you not think that was a bit harsh, Laird?"

That comment had Gil spinning around to make sure he didn't miss Alex's answer to the laird. It was a rare event when someone dared to question Alexander Grant. He certainly wasn't fool enough to make that mistake.

MacTear directed his comment at Alex. "Bairns should not be in the hall with the adults, should they?"

Elizabeth did a slow turn and said, "Explain yourself, please."

"Naught to explain, my lady. Bairns can be loud and rambunctious with all their crying and demands, do you not agree? 'Tis their way to behave out of sorts, so keep them out. The elders should not have to witness such behavior."

"Nay, I do not agree at all," she said sharply, her eyes traveling to her mother.

Alex said, "My grandchildren are welcome in the hall. Always."

"As you wish," MacTear mumbled, his hands now behind his back. "'Tis not the way in my hall, but 'tis your right." Then he turned to Elizabeth, who was now glowering at him, and said, "If you don't mind, I'd like to show you the sweet mare I would present to you as a gift if you were to become my wife." He held his hand out toward the door as if to usher her outside.

Gil watched as the woman he loved did her best to hide her emotions. He knew she wanted nothing more than to slap the man for his arrogance. Lizzie adored children and would protect them with every part of her being. To overlook his blind arrogance would be difficult for her, but she would do it so as not to embarrass her parents.

Or so he guessed.

Gil did his best to silently convey to Elizabeth that he didn't wish her to go, but she smiled and lifted her skirts. He bit his lip, for he understood her motivations: she wanted to get rid of the man, and this was the most expedient way. Besides which, he suspected she was looking for more reasons to deny the man's suit. He'd just given her a large one. If she went with him, she was more likely to find another, perhaps one that could convince her mother of his unsuitability. He knew how her mind worked and was often impressed with her intelligence, crafty like her sire, he thought.

He still would have preferred that she not go out to the stables, but he trusted her above all others.

Lizzie's mother approached them before the invitation could be accepted or denied. "I did not hear all with the bairns catching my attention, Laird MacTear. Where are you headed?"

He answered quickly. "I've requested your daughter's presence at the stables. There's a fine mare I'd like to give her as a betrothal gift. I brought the animal along so that she might see her sweet countenance. If you'd like to join us, I welcome you, my lady." He was every bit the gentleman this morn, decked out in his finery with a pleasant smile on his face. Gil wished to cuff him, or perhaps dirty his shoes.

"Nay, you two run along," Maddie said with a slightly strained smile. She took two steps, then hesitated slightly.

Gil, who knew how much she loved bairns, hoped she would chastise the man for his rude comment.

"Mother, is something wrong?"

He hid his grin. Apparently, the same thought had crossed Lizzie's mind.

"Nay, I'm fine, my dear. Go ahead with the kind laird." Something in her expression changed, though, telling him that even Maddie wondered if he was truly a "kind" laird.

Lizzie headed toward the door, only to be stopped by Dyna, who'd just come down the staircase. She cut in front of the laird and held up her hand, palm outward, stopping him.

"What's wrong with the lassie, my lady?" MacTear said, making no attempt to speak quietly. "Is she wrong in the head?"

"Nothing is wrong with her. Dyna is my niece." The way her neck tipped told everyone she didn't care for the laird's question. Reason number two for Lizzie to deny him. She would not like someone questioning her niece's mind or abilities.

He cleared his throat and nodded for Dyna to speak. A moment later, she looked at Lizzie and said, "You'll not like his insides. They're bad, especially right there." She pointed to the center of his chest, then skipped over to her father.

Gil struggled to contain his smile. He had a new appreciation of the wee lassie whose unusual hair was so like her mother's.

"Foolish lass. She doesn't know what she's saying," MacTear said, fortunately dismissing something another man could have been upset about.

Lizzie never glanced at anyone, instead going out the door in front of MacTear. The man seemed innocuous enough, but Gil didn't trust him. Even less so now. As Elizabeth left, her gaze fell on her mother, as it often did. So protective of both parents, Gil knew she would never wish to leave Grant Castle. Hence his agreement to come here. But they both loved Castle Curanta too, and the work that Loki and wife did there was so important that he wondered if they could perhaps split their time between the two castles.

Orvar stormed out of the hall, and as he passed Gil, he heard him growl, "You'll not steal her from me, MacTear."

Gil's insides roiled. This competition could come to a final challenge in the stables, out of everyone's sight. Would they take it as an opportunity to push Lizzie to do something she didn't wish to do? Or force her? It was far from unheard of for lairds to attempt to steal a desirable bride.

Gil pushed his way to the dais, no longer caring how others might interpret his actions. He marched directly to the spot in front of Alex Grant, who'd just returned to his seat after helping Madeline to hers. He felt keenly aware that Alex was Loki's laird, the one who'd gifted Castle Curanta to him.

Without this man, Gil would have had no home.

"My laird, do you think it wise to allow Elizabeth to go to the stables alone with Laird MacTear?" He didn't like it one bit, so surely her sire didn't approve either.

"Elizabeth can handle herself, Gil. You need not worry."

Her mother smiled and added, "He's a fine man, Gil. Please do not worry yourself about how he treats her. Though he clearly holds a few views that contradict our own, he's always been naught but kind. His views about bairns carry no reflection on how he would treat Lizzie."

The palms of his hands were drenched with sweat. "But I believe you *should* worry. And the Norseman disappeared. What if he's out to start a wee skirmish over your daughter's hand?"

"Gil, Laird MacTear is only taking her to the stables to introduce her to a horse," Maddie said. "Our stable master is there and so are many lads. He intends to give the mare to her—if she will finally accept his suit." Madeline arranged her skirt while two serving lasses, in a hurry to attend to their mistress, brushed against him on both sides, serving her a fruit tart and a weak wine. "In fact," she said, "it would please me quite a bit if she came back into the hall betrothed to him. Then the Norseman would leave and the baron would not return. It would put an end to King Edward's attempts to play with our daughter's future. 'Tis none of his concern, in my opinion."

Gil would certainly not be pleased if she came back betrothed, but he also believed it to be highly unlikely. He didn't believe Lizzie would take the façade that far just to please her mother. Lizzie loved *Gil*, not some neighboring laird.

He had to do everything he could to prevent it from happening.

Elizabeth had to admit the offer of greeting a new mare was most enticing. It had been one of her motivations for accepting the laird's offer to go to the stables, although the primary goal was to find as many reasons as she could to refuse him—reasons that would resonate with her mother. His treatment of bairns counted against him, to be certain. One of the things she loved best about Gil was his big heart. No bairn was too small or too stubborn or too broken for him. He gave them all attention, treated them all like family.

"May I call you Elizabeth or Lizzie?"

"I prefer Elizabeth," she said, unwilling to allow anyone but Gil to call her that. It had a nearly sinful overtone to it after all the times he'd called it out during their lovemaking.

"You may call me Symon. If we are to be married, it would certainly be appropriate," he said as he leaned over and gave her a kiss on the cheek.

She didn't like it. It took a measure of control not to wipe it away with her sleeve.

"We haven't reached that point, my lord."

He ignored her, just said, "All in good time, my dear."

All in good time, my arse.

It was a good thing he couldn't read her mind.

They arrived at the stables, and as she turned to allow him to open the door for her, she noticed the Norseman and the man named Sten, who hadn't left after all, coming their way.

MacTear closed the door in their faces.

"She's at the end of this passageway in the last stall." As they drew near, she heard the mare whinny a couple of times.

"She's lonely." Anxious to calm the animal, she let go of her escort and rushed to the end. The horse, a beautiful chestnut palfrey with a black mane and markings, nickered as she came closer. Elizabeth cooed the way she'd learned from her mother, talking softly to the animal, who took to her immediately, nuzzling her hand in search of a treat.

Elizabeth, who had learned her mother's ways long ago, pulled out the apple she'd grabbed from the bin on the way in. "Here you are, sweet lassie. Are you looking for a new owner?"

MacTear came up behind her and said, "Say the word and she's yours." He gave her a broad smile and stepped back as if pleased with himself, crossing his arms.

Puzzled, she continued to pet the horse. "What word is that, my lord?"

"*Aye*. She's yours if you'll agree to be my wife and come to my castle for a visit. Please come meet my clan and see the beauty of my land. You'll love it. They are in need of a wonderful mistress, and you would fit perfectly."

A lightly accented voice said, "I think she'd be better suited to the land north of here. She has the coloring of a Norsewoman, so she'd be readily accepted. I can offer you jewels and handmaidens to take care of your every need." Orvar moved toward Elizabeth, bowing slightly.

Neither suitor seemed to notice the man behind them, who did his best to sneak inside without making a noise. Gil stood to the side of the door, listening to their conversation, but she ignored him, if that were possible.

She had to ignore him. Her suitors were about to show their true character, and she needed to take careful note of it.

Forget the lords and ladies, the dress plaids and shiny boots, what would she find in their hearts when no one was about to watch them?

MacTear stepped closer to Orvar. "You are intruding on our time together, so I'll ask you politely to take your leave."

Orvar stepped closer, Sten entering the stables behind him with his hand on the hilt of his sword. "But you intruded first, when we are at the dais. You cleverly pushed me aside in the hopes the lady and her parents would not dare challenge you, but I do."

Elizabeth caught the slightest of movements from Gil, but she managed to throw a subtle glare his way and motion for him to leave, which he did. Now it was time to address these two fools.

But she didn't get a word out before MacTear gave Orvar a shove and said, "Leave now."

The Norseman shoved him back while his second whipped the sword out of its sheath.

"Do not touch him again," Sten growled.

"Gentlemen, please leave," Elizabeth said firmly, trying to take control of the situation before it escalated.

With a gleam in his eye, MacTear said, "See, the lady has asked you both to leave. Though calling you gentlemen is being too kind."

Elizabeth turned to face him. "My head is paining me. I'd like *all* of you to leave. I appreciate your offer, my lord, but I am not ready to commit to anything. Please go home."

"As you wish, my lady," Orvar said. "I'll escort you back to the great hall."

"Nay, I'll find my own way. I thank you both for coming, but the festival has come to an end. Now, I must go lie down." She left in a whirl of her skirts, leaving them both gaping, no doubt. When she reached the door, she said to the stable lad, "I'll send a few guards to make sure they take their leave shortly."

She tore out of the stables, stopping at the gates before hurrying across the courtyard and into the great hall. When she entered, all eyes turned to her. Gil hadn't been in the courtyard, so she had to wonder where he'd gone, but she hadn't been lying about the growing pain in her head. She was desperate to lie down.

Not wanting to deal with anyone just yet, she headed straight for the staircase. Keeping her head down, she rushed up the stairs and down the passageway to her chamber at the end. Once inside, she collapsed on the bed, wondering what would happen next.

Would the two men return? She didn't know, but she'd had enough of them both. The door opened, and her mother came rushing through the door, followed by a serving maid who headed straight to the chest with a pitcher of water, then added wood to the fire to heat the chamber.

"What happened, Elizabeth?" Her mother sat on the side of the bed, reaching for her hand. "You were with Laird MacTear. Where did he go?"

Before Elizabeth could answer, her three nephews stormed through the door and her mother released her hand so she could greet them.

"We'll protect you now, Aunt Elizabeth," Els said. "We got 'Dair a new sword. They'll not hurt you again."

She sat up and pulled the lads over for a hug, but they each made their own special face of disgust and wriggled away from her. "Aunt Elizabeth," Alick cried. "We're too big for hugs. We're fighting warriors now. No kisses, no hugs." He gave her a stern look that told her he wasn't teasing.

Elizabeth laughed and said, "No hugs then. I sent the men home. You may go to the stables and make sure they've taken their leave. I'll be fine now."

Alasdair's eyes widened as he hurried over to the door. "I'll go first."

"Nay, me!" cried Els.

"She told me first," Alick cried, giving Els a shove.

Elizabeth smirked, glancing back at her mother. "Do you suppose they'll ever stop being so competitive and get along someday?"

"They're bairns," her mother said. "You'll be surprised to see what they'll do as full-grown warriors, I think. I suspect we all will." She stared at the door, the look in her eyes telling Elizabeth just how much her mother loved each and every one of her children and grandchildren. "Why did you tell the men to leave?"

"Mama, my head pains me and they started arguing. I've tired of the competition between the suitors. It was too much for me."

"But didn't you see the gift from MacTear?"

Elizabeth sat up and took her mother's hands. "I did, Mama. She is a lovely palfrey, but he wanted me to commit to a betrothal, and I'm not ready for that."

"Why not?"

She rubbed the crease in her forehead, wondering how truthful to be with her mother. "'Tis difficult to explain."

"Never mind, dear," her mother said. "You need not tell me now. Rest your head, and we can talk later." Her mother got up from the bed and motioned for the housemaid to follow her. "I think she needs some time to herself."

Once they left, Elizabeth sat on the edge of the bed, pondering her dilemma. She had no intention of marrying anyone other than Gil, but her mother was being quite persistent. She moved over to the window, pulling the fur back so she could gaze at the hustle and bustle in the courtyard. Some of her clansmen were headed home, others were busy doing their normal work for the clan. The armory and the buttery were both busy.

Then she caught sight of the train of mounted men leaving together—Loki's group. There sat Gil, looking taller and more handsome than any of the others. It didn't matter that they were so far beneath her, she knew it was him—she'd know him anywhere—and she wished to yell at them to stay.

One more day, one more sennight, one more moon. A tear meandered down one cheek. Her heart ached whenever they parted, especially when they weren't able to say goodbye. Still, she knew she'd see him soon. She would visit Castle Curanta to give lessons to the bairns or bring foodstuffs, whatever tale she chose to tell. Or he may return for a "forgotten" item or to deliver a message. They were never apart for more than a sennight, but still...it wasn't enough anymore. Without Gil, she was lonely, and all of her siblings were married except for Maeve. To her surprise, a knock sounded at the door.

Connor stuck his head in. "Am I bothering you? Mama said you're not feeling well."

"Come in, Connor. I could use some advice." She waved him over to the chair in front of the hearth while she took the other one. "Help me decide what to do."

"I'll try my best. What's the problem?"

She sighed. "Mama wants to betroth me to MacTear." There. She'd said it. He should be able to come up with an answer.

"And you're not interested in him?" Connor drummed one set of fingers on the arm of the chair.

"Nay."

He paused, probably hoping she'd say more, but she didn't. She couldn't, without telling him all.

"There's naught wrong with him, Elizabeth, and you are past the usual marrying age. Do you wish to remain a spinster?"

"Nay, but I'll not marry him."

"Elizabeth, there have been five different men here over the last moon, specifically pursuing your hand in marriage. Granted, the baron was a disaster, but there was nothing wrong with the other four. Sela liked Orvar, though she wasn't fond of Sten."

"Connor…" How could she explain that she loved someone else? That she wanted him more than anyone, but she couldn't marry him yet because she didn't want to leave Grant Castle. Because it did not seem wise or kind to pull Gil away from sweet Sabina yet.

"Is there someone else? Say a name, and I'll talk to Papa about him. You know he believes in allowing you to choose your own husband, and both of our parents would like to see you married." He stood and fussed with the fire, banking more wood.

Almost ready to confess, something stopped her. "Nay, no one, but…"

"But what?"

"I'm just not ready yet, Connor," she blurted out. "Thank you for your help, but I need to lie down."

He gave her an odd look, then lifted her out of her chair, squeezed her, and whispered, "I'm here for you when you are ready to tell me."

What the hell did that mean?

CHAPTER FIVE

GIL BRUSHED HIS horse down in the stables at Castle Curanta, the beast giving him a wee shove with his muzzle as if to suggest he was being too rough. "You are not fooling me any, Thunder. You are just as upset as I am that we left. I think you prefer the lass to me, because she gives you more apples than I do. You are a fickle beast."

The group had arrived home the previous day, but he'd just come in from a long ride, something that had helped him sort through his thoughts.

He could rub the poor horse down for days thinking on all that had taken place at Castle Grant.

Fortunately, the animal did not feel the need to kick him, so he continued with his ministrations on his brown coat. His mind conjured memories of Elizabeth. Several of the Grants came to visit them at Castle Curanta, offering their help, but none of them came as often as Elizabeth. Bella had said it was because she was so devoted to her mother's cause of teaching young ones to read, but Gil had realized after many moons that it was her heart that brought her back so often.

It was her heart that brought the bairns to *her* over and over again.

Ever since Castle Curanta had become a home for orphans and lost children, their numbers had grown more and more each year. Some couples had moved from Grant Castle because Loki needed warriors, but others had drifted here on their own. Families in search of a home, a place to belong, a place where their work would be appreciated. Castle Curanta had blossomed under the leadership of Loki and Bella. Their village had grown, and they'd gained more and more bairns, but they were always in need of warm embraces and comforting voices.

The bairns who'd lost their parents struggled when they first arrived. Their smiles grew during the day, but at night, they were often haunted by nightmares. Bella comforted many, but one pair of arms would only go so far, and so others came to help. It hadn't taken long for the bairns to learn that the most welcoming and warm pair of arms belonged to Elizabeth Grant.

They waited for her arrival and cheered when she came through the gates. Her smile and calm countenance were just what they needed.

After a few moons of watching Elizabeth, Gil had noticed her remarkable ability to draw out the toughest children. The most difficult orphans could be tamed by her love, and everyone knew it.

Love. It was that simple. Elizabeth loved every bairn she held.

He'd always thought her beautiful, remarkable, but things had changed between them last winter at Castle Curanta, when Kenzie and Loki brought home a few orphans from Edinburgh, something they did at least once a year.

One wee lassie had begun to thrash and sob, fighting to be let down from Kenzie's horse. Loki had marched her inside the hall, Kenzie and Gil following him, and handed her straight into Elizabeth's arms.

She had carried the bairn to the hearth, humming a tune into her ear and rocking her. The toddler had continued to fight, he guessed because there was so much going on in the hall. The poor thing looked as if she hadn't eaten in days.

Elizabeth called out to him because he was the closest. "Gil, find us a chamber with a hearth. There are too many people here, then bring us some goat's milk."

He'd done as she asked, finding the chamber and banking the fire in the hearth until it emitted a soft orange glow. Once the two were settled near the fire, he left to fetch the milk. When he returned with it, he knelt in front of Elizabeth's chair. "What's her name?"

"Sabina. Sweet Sabina."

Gil had glanced at the bed and noticed a fabric animal, so he grabbed it and set it inside the lass's arms. She stopped kicking and stared at him, then shifted her gaze to the stuffed lamb in her lap. Elizabeth continued to hum, calming the girl, until she looked up at Elizabeth and then began to pet her arm.

That had moved Gil more than anything else. "She likes you."

Elizabeth had smiled and nodded, resting her cheek on the top of the girl's head. She changed her humming to words. "Even though you've had difficult times, you've come to the right place. We'll care for you, wee one. I promise to love you forever."

The arm caress of Sabina's had become a tight clasp on Elizabeth's forearm, as if she feared she would disappear. Elizabeth motioned for him to fill a cup with goat's milk. He tried to hand it to her, but she said, "You can do it, Gil. She won't let go of me."

The big eyes in the haunted face locked onto his gaze. Her eyes didn't leave him as he gave her small sips of milk. "Isn't she the loveliest sight you've ever seen?'

Indeed, he had to agree, almost. Elizabeth was the loveliest sight he'd ever seen. He was close enough to take in her sweet floral scent, and her luminous skin didn't have a freckle or a mar anywhere. Elizabeth's presence moved him in a way he'd never experienced with anyone else.

It was then he decided he could fall in love with someone.

He volunteered to help Elizabeth every time she visited after that. Six moons later, on a hot summer day, they worked together to help a horse deliver a fine foal. Elizabeth had stood after kneeling next to the mother and newborn for hours, and her knees instantly buckled. He caught her, and for a moment she just stared up at him—then she reached out to grasp his chin and tugged him forward.

He was powerless to stop it, although only a fool would have wished to. The delicious invasion of Elizabeth's tongue had shocked him…and then stoked a fire in him. He'd ravaged her in return, giving all that he got as she groped his arms and chest. It had been a new world for him, sharing something so intimate with someone, and he couldn't get enough of her. He'd had small dalliances with a few lasses, but nothing like this.

No one else could measure up to Elizabeth, in his eyes.

He'd kept his hands to himself just because she was the laird's daughter and sister, but she'd come closer, pressing her breasts against his chest until he had a bulging erection under his plaid that could not be tamed.

She ended the kiss and said, "I've been wishing to do that for a long time, Gil."

To his surprise, she strode out the gate of the stall and glanced back at him, whispering, "I hope for much more another day."

That had been less than seven moons ago. Had he been fortunate enough to see her more often, he'd have fallen in love faster, but they had their restrictions.

Loki pulled him away from his daydream a few moments later. "Gil, I'm going to need you to travel with us to Edinburgh."

He dropped the brush and spun around to face his laird. "What?"

He knew Loki was speaking of the annual trip the warriors of Castle Curanta made to help orphans, but *he* had never gone.

"Kenzie's knee is still troubling him, and he cannot go. I need you to go in his place. Will you be my second on this journey?"

Gil stumbled with his words for more than one reason. His mind struggled with two different thoughts. First, this was the duty he'd always dreamed of, and second, that he was afraid. That same fear he'd always had reared its ugly head again.

As if he could read his mind, Loki said, "Glenn of Buchan and Simon de La Porte are both dead. They'll not come for you again."

Loki knew of his troubles. Although he didn't mind traveling to other places in the Highlands, Edinburgh was the place he'd lived as an orphan before de La Porte found him, and it was closer than he'd like to Buchan Castle, where he'd lived as a near prisoner.

He wiped the sweat from his brow, then said to Loki, "I know they are dead, but 'tis hard to forget. The men who worked for de La Porte liked to taunt me, to threaten to do the unthinkable. I was barely able to understand all that was happening with Kyla and Finlay, much less what they laughed about between them."

Loki said, "I understand your hesitation. Know that when you were four and ten, you could not hold a sword big enough to battle those men to protect yourself. You've trained hard for many years. They'd not be able to challenge you because they'd be on the losing end. Have faith in yourself, though my guess is those men are already dead."

He thought for a moment, understanding that this could give him the chance to impress not just Loki, but possibly Elizabeth's sire and brothers. If he did a fine job, they would know of it, he was certain.

This was a turning point for him. It was time to overcome his fear and grab what he wanted with both hands. The honor of being Loki's second was something he'd dreamed of for years, though he hadn't guessed it would happen this quickly.

He smiled and said, "'Twould be my honor to act as your second, my laird. I'll do whatever you wish of me."

Loki clasped his shoulder. "Good, we leave on the morrow."

Hell, but he'd hoped to see Elizabeth in another couple of days, but he'd be in Edinburgh by the time she arrived.

He had to do it. This was it: his chance to make Alexander Grant see him as something besides a penniless orphan.

Elizabeth had a powerful urge to see Gil. Perhaps it was the bite of the baron, or the closeness of MacTear or the Norseman, but she wished to be in his arms again more than anything. Once that urge started, he was the only one who could satisfy her, so she decided to set off to Castle Curanta before the snow began to fly. She'd head out midday because it would only take her a few hours to get there.

The first thing she did every morn, after freshening herself for the day ahead, was to head downstairs to check on her mother and father. She'd always bring her mother something warm to drink, and her father his giant bowl of porridge with just the right amount of honey. If anyone else prepared it, the taste never quite suited him.

She knew how to take care of her parents. After speaking with them, she would head to the kitchens to find Kyla and Gracie and update them on her plans once they went over the menus for the next few days.

So she fetched her sire's porridge from the kitchen, along with some warm broth for her mother, and headed back into their chamber. She attempted to do it sneakily, hiding from the others in the clan, because they all kept asking the same question.

Who had she chosen?

The answer was simple. None of them.

As soon as she entered the bedchamber, her mother called out to her, "Elizabeth, have you given any more thought to Laird MacTear? Or have you considered any of the others you've seen in the last moon?"

Elizabeth waved her hand and said, "Nay, Mama. I have other priorities today, and my mind will not change about MacTear. I will *always* welcome bairns in my keep."

"Oh, lass. I must agree with you that his comment was unsettling, though I do believe he'd be different with his own bairns."

"I would not tolerate my bairns not being allowed in the hall. What foolishness." She didn't try to hide her disdain for the man. "Besides, you know I must leave for Castle Curanta. Aunt Caralyn said she wished to bring more healer supplies to Bella. I promised to go along with her."

Castle Curanta was her favorite place to visit, and not just for the obvious reason of seeing Gil. Elizabeth helped teach the wee ones their letters and tell them stories. She and her sisters wrote stories for the bairns too, on parchment paper illustrated by their mother. She had two new ones in her bag, carefully wrapped and tied with ribbons because it gave the wee ones such joy to open packages.

Her heart swelled with love whenever she visited. She'd grown quite attached to wee Sabina, especially, and then there was the man who made her heart overflow with love and desire, who made her want to soar into the air and pluck a thousand stars out of the night sky.

"All right, dear. I know you love teaching the wee ones, and it pleases me to know so many of them have learned to read with your help. You've become an inspiration to many. Go along. I don't wish you to have trouble on the road."

"Aye, Mama. As you wish." She kissed both of them on the cheek, then made her way to the kitchens for a basket of treats. The wee ones knew she always came with extra food, and Cook had quite a reputation with pastries.

It was but a two-hour ride on a good day, so she chose ten guards to travel with her and her aunt before donning her mantle, finding Aunt Caralyn, and leaving. Anxious to see Gil, she kept tugging on her horse's reins, urging Midnight Sun to fly across the meadow.

Aunt Caralyn said, "Seems to me you're in a hurry to get there."

Elizabeth shrugged her shoulders, slowing her horse a wee bit. "Sunny loves to gallop, so I like to give her the freedom she wants."

Aunt Caralyn persisted. "Is there someone special there, Elizabeth? Someone who's caught your eye? Who makes all of your suitors fall short?"

Surprised that her aunt was so insightful, she said, "Nay, I just love visiting with Bella and all the bairns. Sabina has caught my heart. I worry about her."

Aunt Caralyn pulled abreast of her. "If there is ever someone, I hope you'll trust me enough to share with me. I know it's often hard to share with your parents, even your brothers, but I'd be happy to help if I can. Even if you just need someone to listen."

Elizabeth nearly bared her soul, but she stopped, aware of the guards around them. "Perhaps someday that will happen. I appreciate your offer as 'tis most difficult to discuss such things with my mother. Maeve is too young to understand, and Kyla keeps so busy."

"I'm always here for you, lass."

She couldn't help but give careful consideration to her aunt's offer. Were it not for the guards, she could consider it. She had a sudden yearning to share their happiness with someone. Kyla? Connor? Aunt Caralyn? That would be the way to start, to share her secret with someone she trusted immensely. Confide in someone she trusted, get their opinion on whether her parents would support a match with Gil.

Convinced this was a good step, she vowed to talk to her aunt once they returned to Grant land.

And the more she thought of it, the more she was convinced that sharing with Aunt Caralyn was a good idea. Kyla was terrible at keeping secrets, and Connor would feel obligated to tell Papa. But her aunt wasn't one to judge, especially considering her...unusual courtship with Uncle Robbie. She was the perfect choice.

She was going to do it.

CHAPTER SIX

GIL AND THORN fought in the lists, to the shouts of all the other guards at Castle Curanta. Loki stood back with a smile on his face, watching them with obvious pride.

"You know I'll take him down, Chief," Gil called out.

Thorn chuckled, never taking his gaze off his opponent, circling him before attacking with his next parry.

Gil stopped him easily, the spark from the clash of their blades sending a whoosh of excitement through the crowd. Gil came back strong, swinging his weapon over his head with a growl, but Thorn easily blocked him.

The crowd yelled, but then a whisper crept through the gathering. Somehow, even though they hadn't arranged to meet or discussed when she'd next visit, Gil knew exactly what it meant. Elizabeth had arrived. He held his hand up to indicate a break, and both he and Thorn swigged some ale, their eyes following the most beautiful woman in the Highlands.

Elizabeth Grant.

The stable lads ran to argue over who got to care for her horse, knowing she would smile sweetly at whomever assisted her. She also had a habit of carrying treats with her. This fine morn, she'd corralled a sack of berries, and doled out a small handful to each of the lads. If he were to wager, she'd brought other sweets along, too. She always did.

But he couldn't be distracted. He needed to impress his laird, to prove to him he deserved the honor he'd been given. The battle resumed, and they started to parry again as everyone watched. In fact, he could almost feel Elizabeth's gaze on his back. But then she disappeared into the courtyard, her boots clicking on the stones as she made her way to the keep.

"Have you tired out already, old man?" Thorn teased, flexing his muscles as Gil glanced at Elizabeth.

"Nay, I never get tired." He grinned, knowing he could easily beat Thorn. Sometimes he let him win, but not today.

Not with her here.

They finished their practice, and Loki declared Gil the winner.

"'Tis as good a time as I can think of to announce that Gil will be my acting second on our next trip. Kenzie will be staying here."

The others congratulated him with pats on the backs and shouted praise, and Gil felt himself beaming. He wished more than anything to tell Elizabeth.

He grabbed a linen towel and wiped the sweat from his brow, then headed into the keep for the midday meal with the rest of the warriors. It was the largest meal of the day, and he didn't wish to miss it. As soon as he stepped inside, Sabina ran to him, her arms held high over her head. "Up?"

Gil swooped her up and tipped her sideways until she giggled with a force that drew everyone's gaze. What was more beautiful than a laughing child? His gaze searched the hall for Lizzie, but he didn't see her.

He settled Sabina on his hip, and she stared at him, cupping her hand on his face to turn it toward her. Only his complete attention would do for the lass. "Ebeth?"

Unable to say her full name, she'd settled on shortening it. Elizabeth found it quite endearing.

"Elizabeth is here somewhere, lass. I'm sure she'll find you soon." He set her down, and she headed to the kitchens—in search of Elizabeth, if he were to guess.

"When are you leaving?" Thorn asked Loki as they made their way in.

"On the morrow. First thing."

More shouts of congratulations as well as jests about whether he would measure up carried across the hall as more warriors entered for the midday meal, but he ignored them, heading to the table where the cask of ale was kept. As he filled a goblet for himself, he let his gaze stray to the staircase at the opposite end, specifically to a blonde who'd just entered. He could always find Elizabeth immediately in a crowd because the bairns gathered around her for attention and for the hope of a wee fruit tart. She had Cook make special bite-sized ones for her to share with them.

"Please don't worry, I'll give you each one."

"But my lady, may I have the red one?"

"And I'd like an apple sweet," another said.

"I'll give you each one, and if you trade with each other, 'tis your choice." She opened the basket and began to place the treats into various size hands, giggling as the bairns exclaimed at their good fortune. He noticed none traded, each tidbit disappearing inside a waiting mouth as quickly as it was handed over. The last one went to the small toddler clutching Elizabeth's skirt, Sabina. "Here you go, sweetling. I saved the best for you," she said, leaning down to kiss her cheek.

"Tan tu, Ebeth."

One of the older lads said, "'Tis most delicious. May we have another, my lady?"

Elizabeth stood up to send the bairns off. "Nay, 'tis all for now. I must help your mistress get ready for the meal. Who wishes to help us?"

Several squealed and raced ahead of her, but she turned and caught Gil's gaze from across the hall, just now noticing the men who'd entered the hall. She'd always had a remarkable ability to stay focused on her task, something Gil struggled with—particularly when she was around.

These were the times he regretted their pact of secrecy. How he wished to act on his feelings and stride across to take her into his arms, sweaty though they were. He'd like to get closer, at least plant a kiss on her lovely cheek.

More of the guards came in behind him, rowdy and raucous, yelling about Gil going on the next journey.

Lizzie's steps faltered as she listened, quietly turning around to hear the discussion better. This was another drawback of their pact. Instead of sharing the news privately, he'd had to let her learn from overhearing the other men.

He sucked in a breath as she made her way over to the group.

"Good morn to you, Loki." Then she nodded to him. "Gil." But her gaze only lingered on him a moment before she directed it back at Loki.

"What say you? Where are you headed?"

Loki clasped Gil's shoulder. "Och, you've heard. 'Tis time for our annual journey to Edinburgh. I've already received reports of bairns orphaned from a recent wave of the fever. We are needed this year."

"'Tis early for you to leave, nay?" she asked. "If you go now, will Kenzie not be disappointed? He'll surely be fine in a few days." From the worried look furrowing her brow, Gil knew she wasn't objecting because she simply didn't wish for him to go. She was worried for him. She knew how much he hated leaving home—and that the trip to Edinburgh would bring back dark memories.

"Nay, Kenzie has asked to stay here until he is better. Gil can handle it."

"But Thorn or Nari would probably love to go along with you, would they not?"

Loki gave her a smug look before he answered. "Thorn and Nari probably will travel with us. But it brings a different question. Is there some reason you'd like me to keep Gil here, Elizabeth?" He crossed his arms and waited for her answer.

Elizabeth, who always seemed perfectly collected, stammered out an answer. "Nay, of course not. If Gil wishes to go, then he should." She glanced his way, but it didn't appear casual. Loki had to suspect something. Would he say anything? If he did, Gil could only hope he'd keep it to himself until later when they were alone.

Deciding distraction was the best tactic, Gil, his expression far more deceiving than hers, said, "I'm honored to go with my laird. Whatever he needs of me, I'll do."

"Well, then nothing more needs to be said, does it?" she asked, shrugging her shoulders. She turned to speak with the bairns behind her. "Play here for a wee bit while I go speak with your mistress. Then I'll come get you to assist us with the meal." She spun on her heel and threw her last thought over her shoulder as she left. "Godspeed to you all. Bring back those poor bairns, and

I'll help care for them."

Elizabeth rushed into the kitchens, nearly knocking Arabella over. "Forgive me, Bella. I should slow down." Her heart felt like it was in a vise. First, she had to get over missing him. That was purely selfish because it was such a laudable cause. The orphans needed him more than she did, and the journey wouldn't keep him away forever.

But he might be gone for Yule. Usually, a group from Castle Curanta would join them for the holidays. She'd come to depend on it.

It struck her that she wanted him next to her for the Christmas holiday. Her mother had been raised English so she'd brought many of their traditions to Scotland, especially the act of decorating. Combined with the Norse Yule traditions, this was her favorite time of the year.

But that wasn't her only concern. She knew the journey would test him—it would bring up his darkest memories, and he would have no one to comfort him. She wouldn't be there with him, and she realized she wanted to be.

Bella narrowed her gaze at Elizabeth. "I couldn't help but overhear. Is there a reason you're bothered by Gil leaving?"

Hellfire. Bella had heard everything.

Elizabeth had managed to hide her feelings for six moons, but suddenly she was falling apart.

"Nay," she replied hastily, hating her lies but unable to tell the truth. "I'm just surprised, is all. I thought Gil feared Edinburgh for some reason." She quickly averted her gaze from Bella's, instead focusing on emptying one of the sacks of food she'd brought onto the sturdy table within the kitchens. "'If he's willing, then I'll say no more."

"I think it has something to do with his past, but the men who tormented him are long dead. There's no cause to worry." Bella helped her put the food away in their pantry, then gave instructions to the serving lasses for the imminent meal. "And give the bairns the baskets of bread to deliver to the tables. You know how they love to help."

The two lasses left carrying trenchers and platters of food, while the third one filled the baskets for the bairns to distribute.

"When are they leaving?" Elizabeth blurted out.

"On the morrow. You could probably travel to Grant land with them if you wish to go home so soon."

"Perhaps," she mumbled, but her objective, she decided, was to convince Loki to take Thorn.

That was her new plan. She had to come up with a reason for Gil to stay back. She knew him well enough to know he'd never share his fear of Edinburgh with Loki. Did he truly wish to go?

She needed to find Gil and speak with him. It was the only way she'd learn the truth of the situation.

CHAPTER SEVEN

ABOUT AN HOUR after the midday meal, Gil said to Loki, "I'm headed to the loch. I wish to bathe before we leave and the sun could go down shortly."

Loki just nodded. "Aye, the stink of you." He said with a grin. "Are you hoping to run into a certain lass who is worried for you?"

He gave Loki a look of dismissal, not wishing to discuss Lizzie with him. "I'd not get very far with any lass, if I smell so bad as you say."

Gil surely did need to bathe after his practice with Thorn, but the bathing spot had also become his secret meeting place with Elizabeth. There were few eyes near the loch, so it was a good place to meet. He'd seen the look on her face earlier, the panic. She was fearful of what the trip would do to him.

He hadn't gone far when he heard Elizabeth's bird call. He changed direction immediately, heading directly toward her location.

Once he was confident they were alone, he replied to her call, and she came darting out from behind a copse of pines, holding on to him tighter than she ever had. He wrapped his arms around her and took in her sweet scent. "I'll be fine, sweet Lizzie."

"Gil," she said, leaning back to lock her gaze with his. "Why are you going? You must be able to come up with a reason to stay back."

"Aye, I could, but this could give me the chance to prove my worth to your sire and brothers. How can I refuse this opportunity?"

"But this is Edinburgh. I know how you fear it."

He led her over to a large rock and sat down, settling her onto his lap. "I have my fears, but I'm old enough to conquer them, do you not agree?"

"Aye, but why go on the holidays? Papa says 'tis the worst time to travel to Edinburgh."

He couldn't blame her for worrying. After all, she knew his story better than anyone. She knew he'd been alone and starving, wandering the streets of Edinburgh, when Simon de La Porte had sent out word that he was offering coin for anyone brave enough to fight a large force coming out of the Highlands. He'd called them an invading force of savages, bent on harming young men, and promised any recruits brave enough to fight them a good life at Buchan Castle, one of the largest castles outside of Edinburgh. He lured them in with the one thing they couldn't turn down—food. Food with the best aroma Gil had ever smelled. He'd been so hungry his eyes had teared up from the sweet smell of gravy and vegetables. Simon de La Porte had suggested they'd feast every day. Breads and cheeses, even peas had been promised, along with chicken legs. They hadn't questioned his size or his age, instead welcoming him along with the young men who begged to fight for them. He'd known what he was doing.

The meat pie de La Porte had given him that first day in Edinburgh was the biggest he'd ever seen, as big as his head it had seemed, and delicious from the first bite to the last. With the promise of more, he followed the man to Buchan Castle.

He didn't realize what he'd agreed to until it was too late.

Since he could read a wee bit, he'd been assigned to work in the castle, ordered to do errands assigned by de La Porte and his henchmen, Horas and Morgan. They'd liked to send him on false errands, and all three had taken swings at him for no reason other than cruelty.

He'd hated all of them.

A few days later, he'd learned the truth—they were to fight the Grants. Becoming a Grant warrior had been a dream of his since he was old enough to understand what it meant. He'd never be able to fight them. He'd requested to go back to Edinburgh.

Simon de La Porte hadn't allowed him to leave. Instead, he'd told Morgan and Horas that Gil was not to leave their sight. They gave him instructions on everything: when to eat, when to sleep, what to eat, and when to relieve himself.

They treated him worse and worse with every passing day. Beating him. Forcing him to sleep in one of the cells in the dungeon, where the rats and spiders lived. He'd had nightmares for many months after he escaped them. Every day in their captivity, he'd been covered with black and blue marks. Eventually he'd learned to keep his mouth closed around Morgan, but it didn't matter to de La Porte.

Everything had changed the day the two prisoners from Clan Grant had arrived. Gil had assisted Kyla and Finlay in their escape, and then Elizabeth's father and Finlay had killed both de La Porte and Buchan.

He'd never found out what had become of Morgan and Horas.

They'd threatened him enough times that he still held a small fear of running into them, even though Loki had said men like them would never have the courage to act alone. There was no need to worry, he'd said, especially since he was no longer alone. He was part of Clan Grant, and there were many men who would fight beside him—who would fight for him.

But Elizabeth knew the truth—he had not forgotten the darkest time in his life. He still had occasional nightmares about the two men.

"Lizzie," he said, kissing her briefly. "I'll not be alone, so I have naught to fear. If I were traveling to Edinburgh without our warriors, I might worry, but Morgan and Horas will not attack me when I'm in the middle of five and twenty Grant warriors. We are the strongest fighters in all the land, and everyone knows it. Besides, Loki reminds me that they are old men by now, and I am young and well-trained. Far better than those two ever were."

She leaned her head against his chest. "Are you sure this is what you wish to do, Gil? I'm sure if you spoke to Loki privately, you could convince him to take another."

He sighed and kissed the top of her head. "I cannot do that. I already gave him my word."

Elizabeth pushed away from him and stood up. "I know I should let you go as you wish, but I'm afraid for you. I've not traveled that far in a long, long time, and I would be hesitant to go to Edinburgh. I cannot imagine what it must be for you. Why put yourself through this at Yule?"

He could see the worry in the creases on her forehead. "Please don't do this. You talk as if we are married and I will be leaving you alone. You know I love you, but we have made the decision to keep our relationship secret for the time being. Unless you are willing to change that, I must go. If you *have* changed your mind, then let Loki know, and give him a good reason not to take me."

She took a step back, crossed her arms, and said, "Nay. I cannot do that. We agreed to wait a wee bit longer. Within a year, we said."

"Aye, we did," he said, reaching for her hands, surprised that she allowed him to tug her closer. "But if our situation has not changed, I cannot refuse my laird. This is his land, and he is the one who trained me. I must honor his request."

Lizzie cursed, something rare for her. "Hellfire, but I understand." She leaned toward him, nibbling his chin. "Promise me you'll be careful. I'll not sleep at all while you're gone."

"You know I will," he said, his lips meeting hers in a searing kiss. The passion she brought to it told him, beyond even her words, how concerned she was about this trip. Sometimes, he couldn't help but wonder if he was nothing more than a plaything for Lizzie, but moments like this told him that she needed him as much as he needed her. When he ended the kiss, she turned and stared out over the loch.

"What are you thinking?"

"I'm thinking about how much I'll miss you. And about how this could be good for you, after all. It will help you conquer them."

He wrapped his arms around her from behind. "My thanks for understanding."

She glanced over her shoulder at him and growled, "But I sure as hell don't have to like it."

They left the next day, but Lizzie decided not to ride with them. She'd told her parents she didn't wish to leave the bairns so soon. Although he'd miss riding near her, sneaking glances at her bouncing bottom, Gil was pleased with her choice. Her sweet way with the orphans was one of the things he loved best about her, and it would be difficult bidding goodbye to her around the others, pretending as if he didn't care.

Sabina took his leaving better with "Ebeth" still there.

When they were just outside Edinburgh, Gil maneuvered his horse next to Loki's mount. The closer they came to the burgh, the more sweat appeared on his palms. Memories had come flooding back to him. He'd lived in the northern part of Edinburgh in a small hut. He'd had a younger sister, Morven, but she also had been taken by the heaves.

Loki asked, "You're remembering, are you not? I'm quite sure you are, but what's coming back? Buchan Castle or your parents?" He cast him a knowing look, and Gil had to remind himself that Loki was only pressing him because he understood. Before being adopted into Clan Grant, he had lived in a crate behind a tavern after he'd lost his parents.

"My family."

"Brother or sister? I've forgotten. Remind me."

"A sister. Morven was four years younger than me. She was the first to take sick, then my mother and me, then Papa." He stared up at the gray sky to keep the tears at bay. "Papa had already buried Mama and Morven by the time I healed. But then he fell ill. I buried him as soon as I was strong enough."

"How long did you live alone?"

"I begged and stole, living in our hut, until some men noticed I was the only one inside. They sent me away, taking it for themselves. I lived in the woods after that, taking scraps of food from wherever I could find it. It wasn't much longer before de La Porte pranced around town promising riches to the lads who joined him."

"Better than what you could steal."

"Aye, I knew when the local taverns threw their scraps away, and I learned to get them before the dogs did."

"A meat pie had to be quite tempting. Brodie Grant had Nicol get me a beef pie and a fruit tart when they needed help." He smirked, and Gil shook his head.

"The power of food on a laddie."

"On a *hungry* laddie. Do not forget that. You survived against the odds."

"May I ask where we are headed in Edinburgh?" The question alone set his palms to sweating again despite the cold. Perhaps he should have asked sooner, but he'd needed to focus on the journey, not the destination. Loki had seemed to understand without being told.

"Aye. My contact at one of the kirks told me they have a group of three bairns. Two lads and a lassie born to the same mother, same time."

"Three? I've seen twins, but not three. What happened to them?"

"The father considered them changelings and set them out in the forest. The mother was daft over it, so she reported it to the kirk. The priest went to get them. They are ours now."

"How old are they?"

"Six moons. The priest named them after Noah's offspring—Ham, Shem, and Naama."

"I hope they travel well. You've done this for many years. How do you plan to get them home?"

"Simple, we'll tie them up inside our mantles and knot up some linen squares for them to gnaw on. Babes love to chew on everything." Loki smiled, but then his expression turned serious. "These are not the questions you wish to ask me, Gil. Out with them. We'll be there soon."

Gil cleared his throat, trying to decide how much to say. Then he decided that if he trusted anyone, it had to be Loki. "Where is the kirk?"

"A short walk from Edinburgh Castle. Fear not, we'll probably not be anywhere near your hut would be. Or did you wish to go to your parents' and sister's grave? Where did you bury them?"

"Papa buried Morven on top of Mama in a grave behind the house. He dug another grave before he became ill, just large enough for me. I only had to dig a wee bit more for it to fit him."

Loki's brow lifted, but it took him a moment to speak. Gil had surprised him. Finally, he said, "Never seen my own grave, Gil. That must have been difficult for you."

He hadn't given it much thought at the time, but now he recalled stepping outside and seeing the cross over his mother's grave, with a smaller cross right beside it. There was no cross over the empty grave, but it had been about his size. It had shocked him, but he'd gone back in to tend to his father, feeding him broth by the spoonful until he passed.

"It was, now that you mention it. But 'twas harder watching my father pass. He was a big man, larger than life, and it was horrible to watch him dwindle away without being able to do anything to stop it."

"Do you wish to visit their graves? I'm sure someone else is living in that hut."

"Nay," he said. "I'm not interested. We'll head to the kirk if 'tis what you wish."

"The tolls are up ahead. Once we gain entrance, we'll find a chamber at the inn and eat before leaving for the kirk. There may be other bairns in need of help in addition to the three babes. I like to make my way around Edinburgh for a wee bit. I know where to look for the wee ones with no homes. We'll spend a night or two checking the area. Bella always has a list of supplies for me to bring back, as well."

He nodded his understanding as they approached the line for tolls. The royal burgh teemed with visitors, many going to the marketplace for goods and food, but the line was surprisingly short.

Before they went through, Loki split the warriors into groups, "Take a break," he said to the larger contingent. "I'll only pay the toll for five to come along. The rest of you will stay out here and await our return by nightfall. There's a kirk on the outskirts where you can shelter in the stables."

They reached the toll collector, paid their fee, and moved their smaller group into the burgh. The castle sat atop a hill, its spires from the towers seeming to touch the sky. It was the only building visible from every point in the burgh. Memories of Gil's younger days washed over him, not all of them bleak.

The best memory he had was of snuggling his head against his mother's soft bosom when he was a laddie. She'd always held him tightly when he was sick, or when he struggled to sleep at night.

They left their horses at the public stables, then headed down the path toward the inn that would have chambers for them, moving past vendors hawking everything from chicken legs to weaponry.

"You don't wish to purchase anything?" Gil asked, four of the guards moving with them while the fifth stayed behind to see to their horses.

"The inn is at the end of this path, so if you wish to purchase anything to bring back with you, 'tis the time to do it. I plan to pick up a few small things for Bella. I'll get our extra food supplies on the way out."

He wished to bring home a gift for Elizabeth, but he knew he couldn't purchase anything, or Loki would be suspicious. He glanced at the slippers, ribbons, and woolen hosiery, but nothing looked so fine as what the craftspeople in Clan Grant made, so perhaps there was no need to feel guilty for not buying anything.

Then he saw a booth full of scented soaps, wrapped up in ribbons with decorative flowers tied atop them. Lavender. Elizabeth loved lavender. Loki strode right over. He selected various soaps before making his purchase and moving on to the next booth, which prompted Gil to quickly make his purchase and tuck the soap into the pocket inside his mantle. Loki hadn't noticed, and the men were off talking with a group of strumpets, so they paid him no mind.

It wasn't until they were two booths down that Loki said, "I still smell that lavender. 'Tis quite a strong scent." He looked at Gil with a smirk on his face.

"Did you not buy lavender for Bella?" Gil asked, pointing to the large package wrapped in twine.

"I bought many scents, but not lavender. 'Tis most odd."

Gil ignored him, and they moved on to the next booth.

Then the strangest thing happened.

The man behind the booth looked an older version of the man he feared most—Morgan.

CHAPTER EIGHT

ELIZABETH TUGGED ON the reins of her horse as they headed back to Grant land. Her brother, Jake, had insisted on sending Magnus, his second, to escort her back. They normally traveled around her, keeping her toward the middle, but every now and then she liked to move out on her own for a time. She hadn't gone far when Magnus pulled ahead of her, motioning for her to fall in behind him, and the other guards immediately fell in around them.

It didn't take her long to figure out why.

The baron who'd bitten her lip was headed directly toward them. He was surrounded by about twenty of his own guards, though none had the skill of the Grant guards.

"I'll handle this, Elizabeth," Magnus said. "He'll not come near you."

Elizabeth did not argue with him, because if he said the baron wouldn't bother her, then she believed he would do everything in his power to make it so. She simply remained behind him, awaiting his interaction with Baron Haite.

"You are going in the wrong direction, Baron, are you not?" Magnus bellowed. "England is that way." He pointed to the area behind the baron's group. His reply received a few guffaws from the Grant warriors, cut short when he turned and gave them a look. All turned silent immediately.

"I have found what I came for. I'm here to escort the lovely Elizabeth Grant to England so she can visit my land. Elizabeth—" he nodded her way, "—please join us. You'll not need your guards. I know we'd agreed for you to visit in a fortnight, but I am anxious to have you by my side, so I came looking for you."

"I made no such agreement with you," Elizabeth objected.

Magnus moved his horse back and stilled her by taking her hand. "Do not give in to his trickery. I know how his kind use lies to manipulate people. We will not fall for it." His next comment was louder and aimed at the baron. "She'll not being going with you, nor will we be leaving her side. We'll escort her back to Grant land as we intended. Now, move your horses and kindly allow us to pass." Magnus's horse, Midnight Run, began to prance a wee bit. A powerful warhorse, his stallion was a descendant of Midnight, Alex Grant's favored horse, just like her mare.

Midnight Run snorted at the closest English horse, so Magnus allowed him to put on a show, prancing around the smaller horses ridden by the baron's men. Jake and Magnus had trained the horse to be one of the prized few that relished battle. It took a strong relationship between horse and rider to gain such loyalty.

The smaller mounts began to stir, showing their fear of the huge stallion.

The baron ignored the horses. "I've just come from Grant land, and I have Alex Grant's blessing to escort his daughter to my land. Step aside, or we'll take her by force."

Magnus allowed Midnight Run to rear up onto his hind legs, a sight that frightened most. When his paws hit the ground again, Magnus wore a wide grin. "Baron, shall we go face to face with our swords, or is it to be a battle between my men and yours?"

The baron paled but he did not back down.

The sound of horse hooves behind the baron caught their attention. Jake Grant came barreling toward them on horseback, accompanied by another fifty Grant warriors. He forced his way through the baron's cavalry.

None of the men or horses was quite fool enough to challenge Midnight Rider, her brother's mount. Jake brought his stallion up next to Elizabeth's mare, his presence immediately calming her. "I spoke with my father after we detected your men near our land. I'm here to tell you she goes nowhere with you. And I don't think your group is ready to fight sixty of our warriors, but I can arrange it if you'd like."

The baron's fury showed in his face, his untethered temperament making Magnus break into a wide grin.

Jake showed no emotion, having learned his stoicism from their father. Riding the horse tall, he reminded Elizabeth so much of their father, his long, dark hair blowing in the wind of the Highlands. Taller than any other rider in either group, he looked as if he were in charge of all the Highlands.

Indeed, she guessed he was.

The baron's gaze narrowed, but he spoke only to Elizabeth. "I'll arrange for a special vehicle to bring you to my land, my dear." Turning to Jake, he added, "This is not over."

"Aye, it is. Go home and stay there. You're not welcome here." He lifted his brows. "Or did you wish to go with him, Elizabeth?"

Pleased he'd remembered to ask her opinion, even if the answer was obvious, she replied, "My thanks for your attention, Baron, but I'll be returning to Grant land."

The baron turned to his men, and they moved their horses to allow Elizabeth to pass. Jake led the Grant warriors while Magnus rode next to her, indicating which men he wanted protecting her other sides.

Nothing was said until they arrived back on Grant land. Then Jake moved his horse abreast of hers so they could chat. "Hell, lass, can you not just choose a husband? 'Twould settle things quickly." He grinned at her. "We didn't have to do this much to protect Kyla."

"Kyla ran off to the Lowlands all by herself, so I'd say you did not do well at protecting her." Elizabeth did her best to hide her smirk. Her brother was a fine laird, but he was not perfect, and she didn't mind reminding him once in a while.

Magnus snorted.

"Magnus," Jake said to his best friend. "You have something to say? If I recall, you were busy lifting the skirts of your wife when I was trying to find Kyla."

Magnus threw his head back and guffawed. Everyone knew that Magnus's wife, Ashlyn, had nearly brought him to his knees. He wasn't ashamed of it, either. Now he had a wee daughter and a son who controlled him more than anyone, and Magnus enjoyed every minute of it.

Elizabeth laughed with him, enjoying this chance to tease her brother and his friend. Although she wasn't the youngest in the family, she'd always been coddled and treated as younger than her years, and she loved this glimpse of her brother's playful side. Jamie was quite vocal, but Jake had always been more serious.

But when Jake laughed, everyone laughed with him.

They hadn't gone far when their father approached them on horseback. Jake rode up to meet him, stopping in front of him. "Papa, all is well?"

"I couldn't hold back. Tell me that bastard did not truly think he could whisk my daughter off our land without anyone stopping him." He glanced over at Elizabeth and asked, "Daughter, you are hale?"

"Aye," she replied, not saying anything more because she knew he would wish to speak with her privately.

"Magnus, he approached you asking for her?"

"He did," Magnus explained. "He intended for her to travel with him, escorted by about a score of his own men, as if those poor excuses for warriors could protect her. He demanded we turn her over, said he'd spoken with you and had your permission."

"Liar." That one word was all her father said before he turned his horse around and headed back toward Grant land. Upon reaching the castle gates, he turned to Magnus and his men and said, "My thanks for returning my daughter safely."

Magnus nodded. "'Twas our honor, my laird."

Jake was the one who helped Elizabeth at the stables, and they walked together to the keep. He said in a low undertone, "Do not downplay this, sister. You must be truthful about the baron's threat."

Jake held the door for her, nodded to their sire and, much to Elizabeth's surprise, left.

Her father pointed to the solar he shared with her brothers. Before they could reach it, Elizabeth's mother came out of the kitchens and stopped short. An unwritten communication passed between her parents—her father telling her mother without words that he needed to speak to Elizabeth before she could be properly greeted—but he stopped at the door to the solar and said, "Speak to your mother and tell her you are well."

She did as he asked, hurrying over to give her mother a hug and whispering, "I am fine, Mama. I'll explain later."

She ducked into the solar in front of her father, sitting in the chair she usually took, and he closed the door behind him. "Tell me everything."

She related the events of the afternoon while her sire paced the solar.

"What is it, Papa? Jake sent him away and told him not to return."

"I know men like the baron. To him, this is not over. My guess is he said that to Jake before he left. Did you hear any such threat?" He stopped to see her response.

She swallowed hard because she hadn't put much stock in the baron's statement. "'Tis exactly what he said."

"As I suspected, this is not over, Elizabeth. You'll have to be verra careful from now on. You'll not travel outside the gates alone for any reason, even to run your horse. Understood?"

The bastard was going to make her life hell.

CHAPTER NINE

GIL STAYED A distance behind Loki, in the hopes he wouldn't keep commenting on the lavender aroma wafting from his purchase. Though he did his best to focus his thoughts on Lizzie, he failed. His mind couldn't stop returning to the man he'd seen back at the vendor stalls. Could it have been Morgan?

He hadn't gotten a really good look at the man, so he'd convinced himself he was wrong. He'd jumped to conclusions because his fears and emotions were driving him, something a warrior should never allow to happen.

He blamed the entire event on his imagination.

Either way, the possible sighting had distracted him more than he wished to admit. So when two lads boldly pushed through Loki, Thorn, and Nari, they were taken totally off-guard. Gil was the only one who noticed that one of them snagged a bag of coins from Loki's pocket.

"Loki, your coin!" Gil shouted, racing after the lad of around seven winters.

Loki must have finally noticed because he was suddenly directly behind the lad. The two lads had run off in different directions, but Gil and Loki stayed with the wee thief. Nari and Thorn took off after the other.

He led them down a deserted pathway surrounded by trees. It was Loki who caught him, grabbing his collar and lifting him off the ground into the air. It wasn't long before Thorn and Nari found the other one and dragged him over, cursing and kicking.

Loki placed his hand on the hilt of his sword and said, "Both of you on the boulder and do not move."

The moment they saw his weapon, they backed up with no further complaints. "Return my coin, you wee thieves," he insisted.

"I dinnae know him," the first one said, glaring at the younger one as he crossed his arms.

"The hell you don't. He is your partner in crime. Return my coin." Loki leaned forward, using one of his favorite intimidation tactics.

The lad shook his head vehemently. "I have no coin. I know no' what ye're talking 'bout."

Loki motioned to Gil, and the two picked the lad up, Loki grabbing his hands while Gil took his feet, and shook him. Nothing happened. Loki made another motion to Gil, who hoisted his feet higher, turning him upside down until the coin bag fell from his trews.

"You wee thief. I know 'tis my bag because it has my initials sewn in it." Loki picked it up and made sure the coins were all inside before indicating to Gil that he could set the lad down.

"Why are you stealing?" Loki asked. "Where are your parents?"

"We don't have parents." By the look of their grimy faces and dirty clothing, Gil had to believe he was telling the truth. "Who needs them anyway?" He cast a disgusted look at Loki.

"Tell me the truth about why you're stealing. I'll feed you if you're hungry, but even growing lads like you don't need this much coin to eat."

Loki planted his feet apart and stood in front of the one who'd taken his coin, his arms crossed. The lad joined his friend back on the rock.

The smallest of the two, a lad with red hair and freckles, started to cry. The older one said, "Shush, you wee bairn."

The lad bawled on, sputtering out a few words they could make out here and there. "Kill…catch us…dinnae want….to die."

"Lad," Thorn said, moving closer. "We'll not kill you. We were all orphans, too."

The older one looked flummoxed by the news, but the small one kept wailing. "They said if we make enough coin for them, they'll take us to a nice place for orphans."

Gil was surprised to hear that word of Loki's work had traveled all the way into Edinburgh, though they did journey there at least once a year. It infuriated him to think they'd been used as incentive for thievery, especially since he had little doubt the men behind this had no intention of following through.

"Stop," he said to the laddie. "We'll not kill you." Hearing him carry on so tore a hole in his heart. Though he'd been older when his family had passed on, closer to the older one's age, he'd felt like the wee lad in front of him.

Alone with no one to help him, no one to feed him, no one to talk with. He wasn't surprised to see the wee one with the older one. What would have happened to him otherwise? "How do you know each other?"

"I protect him," the larger boy said. "He's too small to be alone. And there are really mean people out there."

But the wee one kept sobbing.

Finally, the older one said, "He's not afraid of you killing us."

"But I am afraid," the small one said, sniffling. "I'm afraid to die, even if you're not. I'm afraid of all of them."

"Out with it," Loki said firmly. "Who are you working for and who do you fear will kill you?"

The thief finally said, "Will you buy us each a meat pie if we tell?"

Loki nodded.

"We work for a man who lives in a castle beyond the walls, from far away. He leaves men in Edinburgh who watch over us and make us steal. They feed us, but hardly enough. My belly is always growling."

Gil recognized what the lad wasn't saying. "You give the laddie some of your food, do you not?" He would have done the same.

The lad continued, "We never see the man in charge, but he tells the others whether or not to beat us. Some of them beat us whenever they wish, though. They don't care if we deserve it or not."

Simon had been like that. He'd never understood what set him off—if he'd known, he would have stopped the behavior. Eventually, he'd decided the bastard swung out whenever he was angry, and he didn't care who he hurt.

"So we steal," the lad said. "My apologies to you."

Loki looked from Gil to Thorn and Nari. "Sounds familiar. I

recall men trying to make me steal, but I always got away from them."

"We'll take you with us," Gil blurted out, remembering a time when he'd wandered these streets, alone and desperate. Remembering where he'd ended up before finding the Grants. He didn't want that for these lads. "We live in a castle for orphans. ''Tis as we said. We're all orphans."

The wee one stopped crying and whispered, "Ye will? Who runs the castle?"

"They're telling you lies," the thief said. "I've asked the nuns, and they said the only place they know that takes in all orphans is Castle Curanta, way up in the Highlands. She thought there was another one, too, but it's even farther in the Highlands."

"Mayhap they are not lying, Daw," the wee one insisted.

"Shut your mouth, Herry," he replied.

Loki smirked and asked, "What else do you know of that castle?"

"'Tis run by Loki, the orphan adopted by the Grant warriors," Daw said with wonder. He was such a good fighter in the Battle of Largs that the Grants gave him his verra own castle. He was adopted, and now he's a Grant."

Daw, who had dark hair, turned to Herry, whose red hair looked nearly brown from the dirt. "'Tis where we wish to go, but we don't know how to get there. The one man said he'd take us there once we steal enough for them."

Loki had a smug grin on his face, and he gave Gil a slight nod. Tempted to grin himself, Gil said, "Did you look at the initials inside the bag you took?"

"I cannot read letters," Daw barked.

"I can," Herry volunteered. "My Mama taught me my letters afore she passed from the fever. I was just beginning to read. May I look at the letters, my lord?" Herry asked.

Loki held the bag out for the lad, holding the initials up to his face. His eyes widened, and he slowly lifted his gaze to Loki.

"Aye, Daw. It says what you think it does."

"What are the letters?" Daw asked.

Herry whispered, "L for Loki and G for Grant."

"You read them correctly, lad. My dear lady sewed them carefully inside all my bags. My name is Loki, and I lived in a crate behind a tavern in Ayr before the Grants came along and took me with them."

"You were truly adopted by the great Alexander Grant?" Daw asked, his ill temper washing away as awe filled his eyes.

"Nay, I was adopted by his brother, Brodie, and his wife, Celestina. They are my adoptive parents." He sat down on a nearby boulder and rested an elbow on his knee. "But 'twas Alexander Grant who gave me Castle Curanta."

"And every year we come to Edinburgh for orphans," Nari added. "We'll take you with us if you wish. You can live in our castle."

Herry ran over and hugged Nari. "I want to go. I hate those men."

Then he glanced back at Daw for his reaction. He didn't answer quickly, instead slowly taking the measure of each of them. After a long pause, Daw said, "We'll both go, but only if you train us to be Grant warriors."

"Deal," Loki said. "Anything else you need?"

Gil did his best not to laugh at Loki. He knew how to handle young lads. He sat down on a log, memories washing through him. After he'd gotten Kyla back to Cameron land, Chief Cameron had taken him right into the kitchens and told him he could eat whatever he wanted. Gil thought he'd landed in heaven. Cameron keep had impressed him, but not as much as Castle Curanta.

The first time he sat at the trestle table with the other lads and lassies, they shared how they'd lost their parents. Loki came along and told them his story, something that made him realize he was finally where he belonged.

He'd made fast friends who'd never deserted him, Kenzie being his first. Kenzie had taken Gil along everywhere for the first fortnight, showing him everything. To this day, he was still Gil's closest friend.

"Grant plaids," Daw shouted excitedly. " Can we wear Grant plaids?"

"I'll have our seamstress fit them to you. And new trews for winter, along with a tunic or two."

The first time Gil had donned a Grant plaid and gone out to the lists to train, he'd finally felt as if he belonged.

Herry swiped the tears from his face, leaving a dirty streak across one cheek. He held his foot up and asked, "May I have new boots when we get to the Highlands, my lord?"

Gil was caught by the sight of the lad's toes pushing out of the seam of the boot toe. "Nay," he said, before Loki could answer. The lad was about to start crying again when Gil knelt down in front of him. Up close, he'd guess him to be no more than five winters. "Nay, Herry. We'll get you the boots now. I'll take both of you. You'll need good ones to get to the Highlands. And new woolen hose, too."

Eyes shining with tears and happiness, Herry jumped up and hugged him.

Thorn added, "And we'll protect you from the cruel bastards who forced you to steal."

"I promise no one at Castle Curanta will beat you," Loki said. "Ever. What say you? Say aye, and we'll head to the meat pie vendor."

Herry nodded quickly, while Daw took several seconds to agree. But he did it with a smile.

Once they filled their bellies, Loki strode down to an inn, entered, and said, "We'll be staying the night. One large room with four pallets and two for the wee ones." Thorn had held back to speak with the guards, making plans for the warriors to sleep in the town stables.

The innkeeper stepped away for a moment, and Herry pulled on Loki's shirt and whispered, "We don't have to sleep in the stables this eve, my lord?"

Loki patted the top of his head and said, "Nay, lad. From here on, we'll keep you warm each night. Sometimes we huddle in a cave together, but you'll be you warm."

Gil swore he saw tears misting the bairn's eyes. While the other had toughened, this lad clearly had not.

As if Loki could read his mind, he whispered over his shoulder. "Poor lad stayed with them for protection and to stay alive is my guess."

Gil held his hand out, and it surprised him how quickly Herry grabbed it. He led him over to the hearth, the crackling flames inviting in the chilly front chamber only meant for welcoming guests.

Once the innkeeper returned and the arrangements were finalized, Loki nodded to the man. "We'll return, but we're heading to the bathhouse first." Then he turned to glance at the lads, one at a time. "You smell. Both of you. Grant warriors don't smell."

Gil was distracted right away, memories of Sabina fresh in his mind. A vendor with fabric animals was straight ahead so he knew what he had to do. He reached the stall and picked up a gray dog who looked like a deerhound, paid for it, and handed it over to Herry, whose face lit up. "For me? May I keep it?"

"Aye, 'tis yours, lad. Daw, you need one, too?"

Daw, looking quite offended, said, "Nay, I'm too old."

Loki, Gil, and Nari headed down the street with two lads lagging behind—until Loki stopped and said, "You two walk between us. We cannot protect you if we know not how far back you are."

There was a growing cluster of men between the colorfully festooned merchant stalls, so each of them grabbed one bairn and tugged them in tight.

Gil traveled with Herry, who had started to shake. The lad's eyes darted around them, as if looking for an attack he felt sure was coming. "Do not worry, lad. I'll protect you."

No sooner had he said it than a band of six men shoved their way through the crowd. Herry's hand shot up and pointed at two men headed directly toward them. "There they are!" The lad nearly bolted, but Gil lifted him up and pulled his dagger, waiting to see if they would cause any trouble.

A sharp jab caught him in the hip, and he let go of the lad, spinning around just in time to see a man with a bloodied dagger run away. The first thing that popped into his mind was the blood. Whose blood dripped from that dagger?

Herry shouted at the top of his lungs, and Loki, Nari, and Thorn drew their swords and struck down three men coming at them with weapons drawn, but Gil struggled to draw his sword.

Then he found out why.

It was his blood, dripping a river down his leg.

He fought a sudden spell of dizziness by dropping his sword and reaching for the first person he could, surprised to see Daw on one side of him. Herry was behind him, pushing on his uninjured leg. "Go over there," he cried, pushing him while the other two took one arm each and led him to a tree off to the side. He staggered, grabbing onto the bark and leaning his forehead on the tree, attempting to overcome the dizziness. Unable to get his bearings back completely, he crumpled to the ground between the tree and a bush, far away from the melee, though it appeared to be clearing.

"I'll get Loki," Daw said. "They've chased all the bad men away."

Before he left, Daw bent over and pulled a long strip out of nowhere. "Here. You must bind it to stop the blood from flowing."

Gil stared at the lad, unable to put together why he hadn't thought of that himself, but he did as suggested, taking the strip and holding it tight against the wound, which appeared to be in his upper leg, not his hip as he'd originally thought. It was just ahead of the midline of his body, so he was able to reach it, but it was too wide an area to tie around. He'd have to push hard to stop it.

Daw returned quickly with Loki, the others behind him. Loki took one look at him and said, "Thorn, get the saddle bag I left in the inn and meet us at the bathing house. Bring a change of clothing for him and the healing poultice."

Loki helped him stand, but the blood started to flow heavier again, and he cursed under his breath. "Loki, I'll be fine. Do not concern yourself. Put me in the bathing chamber and go get boots for the lads."

"Nay, I'll not be leaving you, Gil. This will take buckets of water to cleanse, then we must find a healer to stitch it. I'll get you cleaned up while the lads wash themselves. Thorn can assist me, and we'll send Nari and some of the guards to search for a healer."

Thorn, directly behind him, said, "You should send for a Grant healer. He'll need a good one."

"Nay, anyone should be able to sew that."

"Loki, I've assisted Bella in her stitching sessions. She says it takes special talent to sew up a wound like that."

"Bella said that? A wound is a wound."

Thorn took a deep breath and said, "I'm not sure exactly, but it has to do with where the wound is located. He'll not be riding a horse easily without popping the stitches. Jennie taught Bella to sew big wounds like that in layers so they'll hold."

Loki picked him up and carried him to the bathing house not far away, which was thankfully close, ordering a tub and a private area. Once the heated water was brought in, Gil stripped down and they poured water over the wound, Gil putting pressure on it. The bleeding slowed, so he took a linen and held it over his private area, allowing Loki and Thorn to take a better look at the wound.

Loki shook his head.

"What the hell does that mean? Am I dying?"

"Nay," Loki said, "but you'll need quite a few stitches. We'll find you some strong ale. I'll send a messenger back to Grant land so they know why we've been detained and what has happened. I hope Nari finds a good healer."

When Gil finished dressing, he sat on a stool and leaned against the wall, still applying pressure to his wound. The lads ignored him because now that they were in a large tub in front of a hearth, they were laughing and splashing like they enjoyed it. He could feel the sweat bead across his brow, the truth of what happened had finally penetrated.

Nari returned with the saddle bag, then said, "The innkeeper told us where to find the healer."

"Good," Loki said. "Bring them to the inn. We'll be there soon." He finished bathing, dressed, and knelt in front of Gil. "Did you see who did it? After you were injured, Thorn, Nari, and I only got in a few swings before the rest took off in a run. It was as if they'd accomplished their objective. I don't think they were intent on killing us all, mayhap just scaring us away from Edinburgh. That could be for any number of reasons. Know you someone in Edinburgh who would wish to stab just you, or do you believe it was an attack on the Grants?"

He shook his head, trying to ignore the thought that would

not leave him. If Morgan or Horas had recognized him, would they try to kill him? He'd told himself it wasn't Morgan he'd seen in the booth, but perhaps he'd been wrong.

Was it possible his old enemy had stabbed him?

"Were you carrying much coin?" Thorn asked,

Hell, he'd forgotten that. He felt in his dirty plaid and discovered his bag of coins was indeed missing. The soap he'd bought for Elizabeth was gone too.

He closed his eyes and cursed. "Simple thievery. My coin bag is missing." He'd hoped to bring her a gift, but now he'd be content just to make it back to her.

Then it dawned on him—just as he'd always feared, something terrible had happened to him because he'd returned to Edinburgh.

He'd been right all along.

CHAPTER TEN

ELIZABETH WAS BRUSHING her horse down when the four guards arrived. Her heart lodged in her throat because she was quite certain they were guards from Castle Curanta. Stepping out of the stables and hastening to the gate, she listened for their request.

"Loki sent us to advise Jake and Jamie that he's been delayed. Gil was injured and is in need of a healer. Once he's stitched, they'll return."

Elizabeth's stomach dropped to her toes. "Gil is injured?" she asked, walking into view. She did her best not to sound overly anxious, no more than anyone else would. "What happened? What type of injury?"

"Sword wound to his leg. Since Grant Castle is closer, Loki was hoping the lairds would send ten guards to Edinburgh. He thinks it was a random attack, but in case it was the baron's men, he wants a larger escort back."

The guard at the gate said, "The lads will see to your horses. Go inside and report to the lairds and grab a meat pie."

"Our thanks. We'll stay for an hour for a brief repast, then we'll head north to Curanta."

Elizabeth hurried back to the stables, tossed the brush onto the shelf, gave her horse a quick kiss, then hurried into the keep, doing her best not to run. Two different kinds of panic warred within her. She didn't feel ready to admit the truth, and yet she had to go to Gil's side. Immediately. Once inside the great hall, she searched for her brothers, but they were nowhere to be seen. Then she heard their voices filtering out from the solar.

She couldn't stop herself from doing the unthinkable—she

barged in without knocking. The look on her sire's face nearly made her step back out to revise her actions, but she held her position, lifting her chin.

Her father's gaze narrowed, Jamie smirked, and Jake stood from his seat, looking perplexed. Her sire spoke in a that low, taut tone she hated, "Is there a reason you entered without knocking, daughter?"

Now breathless from agitation and exertion, she said, "Your pardon, but I heard Gil was hurt. I came to see what I could do to help."

Her father quirked his brow at her. "Do you know more than we do? Is he near death?"

"Nay. Or at least I hope not. I'm here to find out how serious the injury is, and because I would be willing to stay with him if he must remain in Edinburgh until he has healed." Her cheeks heated, and she hastened to add, "I mean to say that I could travel with Bella as a friend to them. Assist them with the stitching, just as I normally do. I'm quite good at soothing others."

Her father watched her for a moment, then said, "Elizabeth, you're excellent at soothing bairns, but I'll not have you out there soothing men's needs in Edinburgh."

Jamie had just taken a sip of ale and spewed it across the desk, part of it landing on the bodice of her gown. He quickly attempted to correct his error. "Elizabeth, forgive me." He carried a linen square to her and nearly wiped at her bodice, but she jerked it from his fingertips.

Her father stood and said to the guards, "Our thanks for the information. I'll escort you to the kitchens for an ale and a meal." Before he left, he turned his gaze to her, and her skin prickled up the spine of her back to her neck and then down her arms, a slow process that forced her to lower herself into an open chair. She didn't wish to meet her sire's gaze. She nearly rose to follow him as was her habit, but he glanced over his shoulder at her. "Elizabeth, you will remain here with your brothers, and they'll make their decision."

She waited impatiently, her mind immediately going to awful thoughts she wished to burn with a hot poker. These were the memories that haunted her most, the ones that prevented her from leaving the castle.

Several years ago, her sire had been struck down in battle. She'd been watching from the parapets, and when her brothers had immediately swarmed in around him, she'd thought him dead. No one had heard her screaming over the parapets.

"He's dying! Help him!"

For her mama had told her she wasn't to leave the parapets. That she was too young to go down below, and she'd been a good lass who always did as her mother told her. So she'd moved up and down the walkways restlessly, helplessly, watching blood pool around her father. Watching her brothers fight, her heart pounding with fear. Worrying that they'd be struck down in front of her eyes, just like her sire, and she'd be powerless to stop it.

When the battle finally ended, her mother had run out and knelt down beside her sire, cradling his head, kissing him, whispering in his ear. Her mother's sobs carried to her over the din as she begged him to stay. "Nay, Alex, nay."

Elizabeth had been close enough to watch as her dear father's eyes fluttered open.

And shut.

And open.

And then her brother Jake had said to let him go.

She'd screamed for them not to listen.

But no one had even heard her.

No one!

A cart had been brought, and Jake had assisted her mother inside, and everyone else had left.

They'd all gone off without her. No one had even thought of her.

Never again would she be a bystander to her family's troubles, forced to watch and not intervene. That was why she ventured no farther than Castle Curanta.

The realization that she'd just offered to go far, far away from her parents to help Gil elicited a sob from her, her body trembling from the force of her emotions.

Connor came in and grabbed her from behind, sitting on a chair and settling her next to him, his arm wrapped around her as if she were a wee lassie. "I know what you're thinking. I can tell by the look in your eyes that you've gone back to that terrible time. You must let it go. We'll never leave you behind again."

Jamie sat on one side of them, Jake on the other. "Papa will not be injured like that again. Your fears are needless, lass."

She managed to stop her sobs, taking a linen square from Jake to wipe her cheeks, her breath hitching over and over again. It just would not stop.

Jamie said, "Do you wish to tell us something about Gil, Elizabeth?"

She shook her head, mopping at her tears and resting her head on Connor's shoulder.

"Elizabeth, he's the only reason you've ever volunteered to leave the Highlands since Papa and Kyla were hurt," Jake said. "It must mean something."

How she wished to tell them all, but if she confessed, everything would change, and that she couldn't handle.

Things had to stay the same. Forever. Papa and Mama safe at home. Her brothers and sisters. Their spouses and children. They belonged at Grant Castle where she could watch over them all.

Connor brushed loose hairs back from her face. "Lassie, we see how you look at him and how he looks at you. That cannot be hidden."

She let out a few more tears over the death of her secret and said, "I love him. Please allow me to go."

Gil gritted his teeth as the healer stitched, keeping his gaze on Loki—pacing behind the healer—rather than his wound. Thorn and Nari sat at the table in the middle of the chamber, the two lads watching the needle pierce his skin, one stitch at a time. Poor Herry flinched at every speck of blood that dotted Gil's skin.

"I'll be fine, lad." He wished to scream to the hills, but he wouldn't let the others see the pain he was in. At least Loki had found some of the sweet amber liquid that took the edge off it. Resting his head back, he couldn't help but wonder how long it would be before he was able to ride a horse.

The healer, a wizened old man with a long beard he had to tuck over his shoulder while he worked, finished by applying salve and a bandage. "Now, you shouldn't ride a horse for a fortnight, young man." He got up and nodded to Loki once he was paid in coin. "If you're in need of anything else, you know where to find me."

The man left, and they all huddled around Gil, the lads closest. Daw asked, "Does it hurt really bad? It hurt me just watching you."

"How would you know?" Herry called out. "You've not been stitched before."

Daw crossed his arms defiantly. "Mayhap not, but my mama poked me with a needle by mistake once. And it hurt like a bee stung me five times."

All Gil could think was that the lads clearly needed some adult guidance in their lives. His gaze caught Herry just before he lost control, tears streaming down his face. He pushed himself off the stool and lifted the wee lad into his arms. "Why do you cry, Herry? 'Tis not your skin."

Herry's head fell on Gil's shoulder. Daw explained, "Herry got bit by a dog once. They had to stitch him. He cries every time he remembers it."

"Ah, laddie," Gil said, stroking his back. "I'm fine now. 'Tis over and you need not worry a bit."

Through his sniffles, he managed to get out a few words. "Must we stay a fortnight, or can we go now?"

"Neither," Gil said. "We must move on, so we'll not wait a fortnight. But I might need to give it a night to start healing before I mount a horse."

Loki sat on one of the chairs and said, "I sent for more guards from Clan Grant. The men I sent will make the request, then continue on to Bella to let her know why we are delayed."

Thorn stepped closer. "What say you about the new guards? They may not be here for two days."

Loki explained, "You and Nari will go to the kirk with me to bring the bairns to the inn, along with any others they wish to send with us. Then Nari and I will bring Herry and any wee bairns back to Castle Curanta. We have enough guards to accompany us. Thorn, you're to stay and await the next group of guards, because I don't want Gil on horseback for a sennight. A fortnight is a bit long, but you must at least wait a few nights. I'll not be burying anyone on the trip back."

Gil set Herry down, and the lad climbed onto Loki's lap, quite content there.

"What about me?" Daw asked.

"I'm asking you two to stay and assist Gil and Thorn until the other guards arrive. He'll need help on the journey home. What say you? Will you stay on as Gil's protector?"

"Aye," Daw said with a smile. His shoulders stood a bit taller as he replied, "I'll help him."

Gil, suddenly a wee bit dizzy, made his way over to one of the larger pallets and collapsed onto it, falling asleep instantly.

He didn't care what happened. He needed some sleep, but then he'd be up and away from this place as soon as he could.

He never should have come.

CHAPTER ELEVEN

ELIZABETH SAT IN the solar the next morn, awaiting her sire's final decision. Though Jake and Jamie had said they'd agree to send her along, she needed her sire's approval before she left. The door creaked open, making her flinch, but it was only Maeve. Her sister stuck her head in, then ran over to give her shoulder a quick squeeze. "You'll find him, lass."

Maeve had the warmest heart of anyone. Her brown hair was always swept up into an odd bun on the top of her head, something Avelina had done for her long ago and she'd liked it enough to retain the style.

"My thanks, Maeve."

She left, easing the door closed, but it was caught by their father, who stepped right inside, Connor directly behind him. While her brother took a seat in the chair beside her, their father sat behind the desk and leaned back in his chair to assess her, something he always did before he spoke to anyone. "You were upset yesterday. Do you have more to tell me?"

Elizabeth sighed, fighting the misting of tears in her eyes. "Papa, I'll tell you all, but I'd like Mama to come in. I'd like her to hear this from me."

Her father nodded to Connor, who bolted out of his seat and headed out the door. "Would you like to say anything to me before your mother joins us? Sometimes I soften things for her."

She thought briefly, then decided it was time to tell all. "I'm in love with someone."

"Who?"

"Must I say?"

"I think you must. I need a good reason to continue to refuse

MacTear and your other suitors." Her father's gaze never wavered from hers. "'Tis also an important piece of judging whether or not this could be a permanent match for you. While my mother believed in allowing people to choose their own spouse, she also believed the family should approve of the choice."

"I'm in love with Gil. 'Tis one of the reasons I visit Castle Curanta as often as I do." She heard a gasp from behind her, only then realizing her mother had opened the door. She turned to look at her, the shock in her eyes making Elizabeth wish to take her words back.

Her father bolted out of his chair and went to her mother, guiding her toward a chair on the other side of Elizabeth. "Who? Who is it you love?" her mother whispered.

She reached for her mother's hand, clasping it between both of hers. Her mother's hands were always cold. "Mama, I'm so sorry. Please forgive me for hiding the truth from you."

"Who?" her mother repeated, her expression one that Elizabeth and her siblings were more than familiar with—one that said don't lie.

"Gil. I love Gil, Mama." Her gaze locked on her mother, waiting to see how she would take this news. The guilt shooting through her hurt like a physical wound, but she had to see Gil.

Her mother leaned forward and glared at her sire. "You knew?"

"Nay, I didn't know until a moment ago, Maddie," he said, lifting his hands. "She does not confide in me." Then he looked to her and said, "I think we deserve more of an explanation, particularly about why you kept this from us, lass."

Elizabeth's eyes misted because she'd known all along this would be difficult, yet it was proving more difficult than she'd expected. She feared they would never accept Gil. Now that she thought on it, perhaps that had been the main reason she'd remained silent all along. Because no was not an answer she could accept. "Mama, it just happened. I watched Gil with the wee ones on my visits to Castle Curanta, and I fell in love. He's so kind, and his gentle manner with the youngest bairns reminded me of Papa."

"Why did you not tell us?"

"I don't know, I was afraid..." Her mind, suddenly muddled, betrayed her, not giving her the coherence she desperately needed.

Her mother finally met her gaze. "All this time, I thought there was someone, yet I clung to the hope that you would find Laird MacTear suitable, just because I am selfish. I don't wish for you to move far away. I couldn't handle you moving to London or Edinburgh."

"Don't you see? 'Tis exactly how I've always felt." She gripped her hands so tightly together they turned a ghostly white.

"You should have trusted us," her father said. "We hold naught against Gil."

"Trusted you? What about the time you were injured, Papa?" She had to remind them of what life had been like for her. Always the bairn of the family, the forgotten one, the one who was left behind. Her father frowned as if he had no idea of what she spoke.

Her mother shook her head. "What has that to do with this?"

The pounding in her head grew, and she jumped out of her chair. "What does it have to do with it? Everything. You left me. Papa was hurt, and you climbed into that cart and left me. I don't think you even thought of me. I cannot live my life like that. I can't be forgotten in another land. The only way for me to know everyone is safe is to stay here. The only place I dare go is to Loki's land because if either of you are hurt, Loki will be one of the first to know."

Her mother took her hand. "Elizabeth, that only happened once, and it was under unusual circumstances. I asked you to stay up in the parapets because I was afraid for you. I was trying to protect you."

"Nay, it wasn't just once. When Kyla was kidnapped, Papa and my brothers attacked Buchan to get her back. They found her in the forest, and you went to be with them. I had to beg to go along with you, Mama." Her tears finally erupted in full, her sobs coming out in gasps. "I'll not be forgotten again, because I'm not leaving you. If Gil and I married, I'd have to live at Castle Curanta." She hung her head, spent from all the crying.

Her father asked, "He would not consider living here?"

"Papa, he says he would—he promised it—but I don't feel

right about taking him away from the bairns at Castle Curanta. He's so devoted to them, and I am too. But I don't wish to leave you either." She paced around her chair, spun in a circle, and then buried her face in her hands.

Her mother stepped forward and wrapped her arms around her. "Elizabeth, we love you dearly. The only reason those things happened the way they did is because you were too young."

"I want to go to Gil. I need to see how badly he's hurt. Mayhap I could stop on the way and ask Jennie to join me. She'd help him for sure."

"But this is far away. Are you going to be able to handle being so far away from us? After all, you just said you could never leave us."

"I am fully aware of how far away Edinburgh is from here, and I would not be going if it weren't an urgent situation." She stepped away from her mother to glare at her father but didn't bother arguing. "I cannot waste any more time. Will you allow me to go? Please? Jamie and Jake said they would, but they want, we all want, your approval."

Her sire looked to her mother, who gave him a nearly imperceptible nod.

"You may go, but with thirty guards. The baron is looking for you, so you must be aware of your surroundings. Do not wander off on your own. Ever. Understood?"

She threw herself at her sire and said, "My thanks, Papa. I love you both."

Gil sat at the table gorging on a meat pie from the tray the innkeeper had sent up. The door flew open, and Loki marched in carrying a one-year-old lad, while a lass followed, cursing and pushing Daw as she came inside.

"I know everything about Edinburgh, and you know nothing," she argued, stepping inside and flopping into a chair with a huff. "I've been here longer."

The lass had fiery red hair that hung in a plait nearly to her hips. He guessed her to be about Daw's age, but it was hard to tell.

Loki grinned and said, "Meet Phillipa, the lass the priest was more than happy to send with us."

"I didn't wish to come with you. They forced me." Her scowl told Gil all he needed to know. She'd lived a difficult life and took it out on others. It was easier to push people away from you than to be vulnerable and try to build a friendship.

This lass had been hurt too much in the past.

"Mayhap if you were a wee bit kinder to those who offered to help you, they may have allowed you to stay," Loki said, handing the bairn over to Thorn, who promptly sat down and fed the wee lad a bit of soft cheese.

Phillipa said, "I go by Phil, not stupid Phillipa. And they are the ones losing out because I know everything in this burgh, so if anything was to happen, I'd be able to help."

Gil arched a brow at Loki, who shrugged his shoulders. "Fill your bellies, everyone, because we're leaving shortly. Only Thorn and Gil will stay behind with Daw."

"I'll stay behind," Phillipa said.

"Nay, take her," Daw argued. "I've seen her about the burgh. She's bossy and pushy."

"See if you like my fist then, wee bairn." She pulled it back in an obvious threat, but Loki set his hand on it, forcing her arm back down to her side, earning himself a fierce scowl in retaliation.

"I'm not a bairn," Daw yelled.

"You need a nipple to suck on?" she leaned toward him, and Daw nearly fell over backward trying to shuffle away from her.

"Enough," Loki bellowed. He lifted Phillipa clear out of her chair. "You'll not be nasty in here. Mind your tongue."

"You said you'd take me to somewhere so I can learn archery, did you not?" She leaned in closer to Loki, clearly not afraid of him at all.

"I did, but not unless you behave." Bending down so they were nose to nose, Loki didn't back down from her either.

"Fine, I'll behave." She flipped her plait over her shoulders.

He set her down next to the chair, and she spat in the corner.

Nari said, "And you'll not be spitting in my chamber."

"Fine," she muttered, pacing in a circle.

Gil sat up and focused his attention on Phillipa. "We'll not be giving you away or leaving you behind, lass. We're not like the others."

He knew how it hurt to be alone, to have no one in your corner, no one whose love you can depend on. To feel you had no choice but to stay with a group of men who enjoyed beating you. It set a fear in your gut that was always ready to reach up and bite off a piece of your throat before you could speak. But he didn't feel that way any longer. Because he had his family from Castle Curanta, and even more so because he had Elizabeth. Something flashed in Phil's eyes, but she didn't respond.

"Eat up, Nari," Loki said. "We're leaving within the hour. We'll take Herry, and the wee lad."

"I thought there were three bairns?" Gil asked.

"An aunt came for them. These were the only two," Loki said, nodding toward the lad and Phillipa. "I'll gather the Grant guards and prepare to leave. The wee one must come with me—I don't want him crying—but the other two can stay here."

"Do what you must," Gil said. "We'll watch over everyone."

As soon as Loki left, Phillipa spun around and said to Gil. "See, even he doesn't want me. You think you can find someone who will keep me? You won't."

"What happened to your parents, Phil?" He decided to call her what she preferred.

She shrugged her shoulders and kicked at a nearby chair. "My sire didn't want me. Sold me to be a housemaid in the burgh, but I ran away. I didn't like the man they sold me to. He had other things on his mind."

Gil didn't say anything, but Daw jumped in quickly. "Touched you where you didn't wish to be touched, did he? Plenty of men do that. You need to take it."

"The hell I do," she shouted, jutting both of her elbows forward and plowing into him, knocking him down.

Thorn grabbed her by the collar and lifted her off Daw, though she managed to get two punches in before he got her away.

"Foolish bitch," Daw said.

Gil let out a loud whistle, and they all stopped to stare at him. When he had their full attention, he said, "We aren't giving any of you away, so quit trying to make it happen. You'll stay with us and take up living at Castle Curanta, the home for bairns like us, who were orphaned or sold by their parents. And you'll stop fighting or you'll get last pick of the food and the beds, wherever we sleep."

Daw calmed down, but Phillipa moved over to the corner of the chamber, hugging herself. "Just don't let anyone touch me."

"I won't. At least not without your permission."

"I want the biggest fruit tarts," Herry whispered, "so I'll behave."

All was quiet until Phillipa said in an undertone, "May I ask a question?"

"Aye, ask all you wish."

She fumbled for the right words, then said, "You know others who were sold by their parents?"

"Aye, I know a few. You're not alone. When we arrive there, I'll introduce you to others with a similar past. Just know that sometimes it has naught to do with you. It has to do with parents having too many mouths to feed or other reasons. I lost my parents, and I ended up in a castle with an evil man who liked to punch my face just for his own laughter. The Grants made sure I would never have to deal with that again."

"Was he big?" Daw said dubiously, eyeing Gil's broad shoulders and large form.

"Aye, I wasn't nearly so big then as I am now, and he was a large man. His name was Simon and he was a mean bastard. But we've no need to talk about him, or about the people who did you wrong. Let's focus on what we can do right. We'll teach you skills like archery and sword fighting, but you'll also have chores. Mayhap working in the garden in summer or shoveling snow in winter. But you'll all work together."

"I guess I'll go with you," Phillipa said, tilting her head in acceptance. She threw a glower at Daw. "As long as this one leaves me be."

Gil glanced at Daw, who was glowering back. "We're keeping you both, so stop fighting for our attention."

"'Tention?" Herry asked, his face quite puzzled.

"Never mind, 'tis not important."

The door opened, and Loki came in with the bairn, a man and a woman following him. "Look who I found along the way.

Maggie and Will."

Maggie and Will were Ramsays, close friends to the Grant clan, the two groups bound together by the marriage of Alex's sister and the former chief of the Ramsays. They were also spies, so it was perhaps not as much of a coincidence as it seemed that Loki had found them wandering about in Edinburgh, particularly since there were ill forces at work in the town. Maggie strode over to Phillipa and knelt in front of her. "Loki told me about you. My name is Maggie, and my parents sold me and my sister to a cruel man, too. But I got away just as you did. I learned to shoot with my bow and arrow, and no man would ever dare touch me now."

Phil's eyes lit up. "Loki promised me I could learn to shoot. Will you teach me?"

"Aye, but only if you agree to get along with everyone. We'll be traveling in a large group. 'Tis important for everyone to get along."

"Are you going with Loki? Because I have to stay with Gil." The look in Phil's eyes humbled Gil, because the hope he saw there was a powerful thing. He decided he didn't wish to know all she'd been through.

Maggie glanced at Will and said, "Well, I guess we're staying with Gil, too. I'd still like to go to the Grants in the end. We haven't visited in a while and I love it there."

"You do?"

Phil had asked the question, but Maggie now had all the bairns' attention. "I do, and so will you. You'll be treated well. And if anyone causes trouble for you, I'll put a stop to it. You'll have many to help and protect you."

"We're heading out," Loki said. "Daw and Phil, you're to assist Gil, get him food when he needs it or anything else he requires. I'm sure Maggie and Will may have to leave for a few hours, so your job is to stay with Gil at all times. And if you do a fine job, mayhap Will might introduce you to his falcons on the journey north. Can you promise me?"

Phil dashed over to Will, her eyes sparkling with excitement. "Are you the Wild Falconer I heard about?" Her excitement spread to Daw, who joined her, staring up at Will as if he were a legend come to life, which, in a way, he was.

"I am, but I doubt we'll use them much until we leave Edinburgh. But I'd be happy to show you then. You must work hard and follow instructions." Will put his arm around Maggie's shoulders.

"I promise." Phil nodded, glancing over at Daw, her red plait bouncing on her back. "I promise to take good care of him if Maggie goes with us," she said, glancing at Maggie with a look of adoration.

"And promise to get along with Daw," Gil pressed. "We can't be arguing in the burgh with the bad men around."

Philippa said, "Don't worry. I know who all the worst men are. I even heard some men talking about kidnapping the finest lass in all the land."

Gil froze, and he noticed Loki stopped what he was doing also. "Tell me what you know," he said. "Who are they planning on kidnapping?"

His mind had jumped to Elizabeth, but surely they wouldn't attempt something so mad. Surely he wasn't right.

"Some lass who is the prettiest in all the land," she said. "I never heard a name."

Maggie smirked. "Will, we have a new venture."

Will gave her a confused look and asked, "What? Who are they referring to?"

"Finest in all the land? It could be someone we know." She gave him a look that suggested she'd thought of the same possibility, which sent fear and anger cascading through Gil.

Loki's eyes widened, and he said, "Find out what you can. You can follow us in a few days, but if Alex hears that, he'll send a thousand warriors to Edinburgh."

CHAPTER TWELVE

ELIZABETH REMAINED BEHIND Magnus the entire way, not daring to move after the baron had tried to steal her away. Connor had pulled her aside before they left, making her promise to do whatever Magnus told her to do.

She'd promised.

Then he'd said, "There's only one part of this that doesn't make sense to me. You said you can't bear to leave Grant land because you don't wish to miss anything, but you are willing to leave Mama and Papa behind to search out Gil. Isn't that a contradiction?"

Their sire had said exactly the same thing. She had to agree with them, but her heart told her to find Gil. To be with him. And she could do no less than follow it.

They talked little because their travel was windy, which made listening difficult, so they pressed along, hoping to make Edinburgh in less than two days. They'd brought thirty guards, so Elizabeth felt quite safe.

They ran into Loki, who was on the way to Castle Curanta with two young lads, and he told them Gil was healing, so Elizabeth calmed her need to get there too quickly for the animals.

"He just needs time to heal," he said, tousling the hair of the wee laddie tied to his chest. The bairn had the sweetest smile she'd ever seen, and she found herself smiling back. "We found a healer to stitch up his wound, but he gave Gil instructions to wait a fortnight before riding a horse. Gil will never wait that long. I gave him instructions to wait a sennight, then we left him in an inn with Maggie, Will, Thorn and five guards." He explained his location. Having conveyed the message, he prepared to ride off, but Elizabeth wasn't satisfied.

She cleared her throat, trying not to be obvious about her concern over Gil. "He's awake and talking? How many wounds?" She had another ten questions but limited herself to the two most important concerns.

Loki gave her an odd look and said, "He'll be fine. He took one good sword slice to his leg, but it's been stitched and patched with poultice, and he's eating fine at the inn. He has a lad and a lassie to take care of him, too." Loki looked at Magnus, who said nothing, then back at Elizabeth. "I'm surprised to see you off Grant land. Some reason you've joined Magnus on this trip, Elizabeth?"

"I'm worried about him, and I thought I could be of assistance. Think no more on it."

Loki gave her a knowing look and appeared as if he was about to say something, but a lad of around five winters interrupted him.

"Is she not the prettiest lass in all the Highlands?"

Elizabeth blushed. "Many thanks to you, laddie. What's your name?"

"Herry. She is, is she not, Nari?" he asked, looking over his shoulder at the man he rode with.

"She could be, I suppose," Nari sputtered, "as she is a beautiful lass."

Magnus peered at Loki for more information. "Thorn will update you." His eyes darted to Elizabeth again. "Have no fear. Gil will survive his attack. They're hoping to determine who stabbed him and why. Whether it was random or for some other reason."

Once they left Loki, Magnus asked, "Do you want to stop on Cameron land? See about your Aunt Jennie?"

Elizabeth considered it, but since he'd been stitched up already, there was probably no need. Loki would have told them if he were in bad shape. "Nay, I don't think we need to. We'll move along." She was most anxious to see him with her own eyes.

Once they reached Edinburgh, Magnus split the guards up, leaving some outside of the burgh and ordering others to patrol inside the gates for any questionable activity. Five stayed with them as they traveled through the town to the inn where Loki had left Gil.

Magnus made arrangements for another chamber, then they headed up the stairs. The innkeeper had told them where the Grant group was, even babbled on about the man's injury in a way that made Elizabeth nervous, so they knew exactly where to go.

Once she found the chamber, she burst inside after a quick knock. Surprised to see Maggie and Will inside talking, with a young lass, she only managed to get out one word. "Gil?"

"He's inside sleeping. I think we may need to call the healer again. He was getting better, but now he has the fever."

Elizabeth had brought some of Brenna Grant's famous poultice for pus-filled wounds, along with plenty of linens for clean bandages, so she moved inside, careful not to awaken him. One look at him quickened her heart. He was in pain. Moving to the one window, she pulled the fur back to allow fresh air inside because the place smelled of illness, a stench she hated. It was as bad for the ill as the hearty, or so her healer aunts had always said.

Perhaps she'd made a mistake by not stopping for Aunt Jennie.

She knelt by the side of the bed, taking in everything about him, saying a quick prayer for the Lord to save him. "Gil?" she whispered.

He opened his eyes and turned toward her voice. "Lizzie? Is that truly you?" His hand reached out and settled on her jawline. She pulled back slightly and kissed the end of his fingertips. Her eyes brimmed with tears she didn't want him to see.

"Aye, I came to help you. Where is your wound? May I look at it?"

"In a moment. Let me look at you first. I missed you so. I dreamed you would come, but I didn't think 'twould truly happen." His fingers gently moved her plait, nearly unraveled from the stresses of traveling, forward over her shoulder. "Have I told you how beautiful you are?"

She nodded, unable to speak the words for fear it would open the dam on her tears. "Oh, Gil." She set the back of her hand against his forehead. "You're burning with fever. Have you been drinking anything at all? You know what Aunt Jennie says. Drink,

drink, drink whenever you're ill."

His eyes fluttered shut, then he forced them open again. "Lizzie, will you marry me? We could live in a hut on Grant land. Or Loki would allow us to live in a chamber at Castle Curanta. Bella would love to have another mistress of the castle. I definitely won't be interested in traveling with Loki again. I said I should never return to Edinburgh, and it seems I was correct. I've made a blunder of everything."

"You didn't make a blunder. 'Twas not your fault someone was after you."

"Aye, it was. I never told Loki, but I think 'tis possible it was Morgan who came after me. I thought I saw him in the market before I was stabbed. If not for me, we could all be home now. I brought bad luck to our journey, just as I feared I would. I knew I should have stayed at Castle Curanta. I never wish to go away again. Only Grant land and Castle Curanta are safe. I felt haunted all the while we traveled." His voice fell off and he looked up at the ceiling. "Lizzie, I'm tired. Forgive me." He closed his eyes and was asleep in seconds.

Elizabeth rested her head on his chest and let the tears flow. "I love you, too, Gil. Please stay strong." She loved to listen to the strong beat of his heart, though it seemed more rapid than usual. Was that a bad sign? She squeezed next to him on the small pallet, resting her head on his chest and wrapping her arm across his belly. The tears continued, much as she wished them to stop. She should go back and speak with Maggie or Will, but all she wished to do was hold him.

The heat of his fever burned against her cheek, but she cared not. Perhaps she should go for help, find another healer, go after Aunt Jennie. The sound of his rhythmic breathing soothed her, as if to reassure that he would be fine, that she only needed to be patient.

Yet his breathing was too fast and not deep enough, the pattern shifting in a way she didn't like. Closing her eyes, she prayed for his health. How she wished she could send him part of her strong constitution to help him heal.

If only there was a way she could flow into him and he into her.

The door opened, and Maggie stepped inside. Elizabeth didn't move her head.

"Is he all right?" Maggie whispered.

"Aye, he just has the fever. He's delirious, doesn't know what he's saying."

"Is there something I should know about, Elizabeth? Is he the reason you haven't accepted any suitors?" Maggie sat on a stool at the end of the bed.

Elizabeth trusted Maggie. They'd been fast friends ever since her sire had forced all the Grant lasses to take archery lessons from Gwyneth Ramsay, Maggie's adoptive mother. She'd gone out to the archery field on Ramsay land, and it had stunned her to see the other lasses' powerful shots. Her sister, Kyla, and Ashlyn had both done very well, in addition to the Ramsay lasses, of course. But Elizabeth was a total failure, and worse, she hated every minute of it. She finally made an excuse and snuck off. "Aunt Gwyneth, I must see to my needs."

Her aunt had nodded as she crept off into the trees, but instead of doing what she'd hinted at, she flopped onto a mossy spot and started to cry. It wasn't long before Maggie found her. She sat down, took one look at Elizabeth, and said, "You hate it."

Elizabeth had cried even louder.

"'Tis not something you need to cry about. Not all the Ramsays are good archers."

"But Papa wants me to do well, and I'll disappoint him if I don't." She sat up and swiped her tears off her face.

Maggie said, "I don't picture your father being upset. Your mother surely won't care because she's never lifted a bow, if I were to guess."

The image of her mother as an archer made her giggle. "Nay, she won't care."

"Then she'll tell your sire it does not matter."

"But all the others are so good at it, and I'm horrible. They'll make fun of me." While she was more worried about her father's reaction to her quitting, she didn't wish for her Ramsay cousins to think ill of her.

"Which one do you think will make fun of you? Aunt Brenna? Jennet? Lily? Bethia?"

Elizabeth stopped her tears, looking up at Maggie with a newfound appreciation. "I hadn't thought of them."

"Aunt Brenna believes in allowing people to choose what they like. 'Tis why Bethia helps heal animals and Jennet started as a healer so young. And Lily? Well, Lily is allowed to be Lily, our own ray of sunshine. Aunt Brenna is your father's sister. If he ignored your wishes and tried to make you into an archer, she would stand up for you."

Maggie had walked out with her, and they'd gone over to Aunt Gwyneth together. "'Tis not for Elizabeth, Mama," Maggie had said.

Aunt Gwyneth had given her a hug and said, "I'm glad you discovered that. You'll find your special talent."

While she still didn't know what her special talent was, she'd learned her family was special indeed.

She trusted Maggie, and it was time to tell the truth. "I love Gil."

"Why aren't you married?"

"Because I'm a fool. I didn't think my parents would approve, and then there's King Edward, who wished to marry me to some Englishman." Of course, that wasn't the true reason at all, but she felt ashamed to admit to the truth. Especially now.

"But he couldn't do that if you married a Scot. Is there some other reason you've kept it all hidden?"

Elizabeth lifted her head and stared out the window. "Maggie, my whole family left me behind after my sire was injured and nearly killed. Something similar happened after Kyla was kidnapped. If I left, they'd never tell me what was wrong with anyone. My mother thinks I have a frail constitution and can't handle bad news. I've argued with her many times, but she persists in hiding things from me."

Maggie said, "Did you ever think that mayhap she was trying to protect you? I see Mama doing the same with Brigid. It's as though they wish the youngest will stay a bairn forever. Aye, I know Maeve's the youngest, but you held that role for a long time before she joined the family, and they still see you that way." She tilted her head, thinking, then added, "And your sire always wished to keep you near. When you were a bairn, you were always strapped to his chest or sitting on his lap. I doubt he's encouraged you to take a husband. Papa does not want Brigid marrying anyone. He growls at any young lad who looks at her."

Elizabeth gave that comment some consideration and found she couldn't argue. Was it possible they'd both wanted to keep her at home? Certainly, her mother had encouraged her to marry MacTear, but her mother had also admitted it was only because he lived nearby. And even though she was three and twenty, this was the first they'd tried to push her into choosing a suitor.

"At any rate, when you get the chance, talk to your parents."

"They know. They didn't say much other than that they would accept him, but my mother couldn't hide her disappointment. She was still hoping I'd accept MacTear. Will you help me with his wound? I need to put this poultice on it."

"I'll get some warm water and supplies from the innkeeper, then I'll help you."

When she returned, Maggie helped her roll Gil over so they could redress his wound. As soon as they uncovered the wound, she let out a low whistle. "I wish Aunt Jennie were here."

Elizabeth felt the color leak out of her as she wiped the wound with a linen cloth. It didn't look good. "I'm going to put this on, and then I'm going for Aunt Jennie. We need her here. His color is bad, and so is his fever. I cannot lose him, Maggie."

"It's not a good sign that he's not waking up from all your ministrations. This has to be painful for him. And I think he's popped some stitches on the inside, stitches that were poorly done. That could be the problem. Jennet would never allow that kind of stitching. Nor would Aunt Brenna."

Jennet was Aunt Brenna's daughter, one of the most talented healers in the Highlands.

Maggie's words were harsh, but then she had always been one for honesty, and in this case honesty was necessary.

Nodding, Elizabeth continued to cleanse the wound to the best of her ability before tossing the now dirty linens in a pile on the floor. Then she applied the poultice and covered it with clean linens, tying them around his thigh.

It had to hurt like hell, but Gil didn't flinch.

Maggie got up and tugged her into the main chamber. "You

are correct, someone must go for Aunt Jennie. Will and I can go, and you can stay with him."

She nodded, her breath still hitching from her tears. Upon entering the chamber, she noticed something was off. No one was speaking, and all were staring at her.

"Phil, what say you?" Will asked.

"'Tis her," said the lassie with a thick red plait. "She must be the one. Golden hair and now that I see you, it makes me think of something else they said. That she is most regal looking because she stands verra tall for a lass."

Elizabeth looked from Maggie to Will, and then to Thorn. "What are you talking about?"

"Phillipa here likes to spy on people," Maggie said with obvious approval. "She's an orphan who's been living on her own in Edinburgh. Before Loki found her, she heard there are men trying to steal the most beautiful lass in all the Highlands…"

"'Tis surely not me," Elizabeth said at once, alarmed. "There are many far more beautiful than…"

"With golden hair and verra tall?" Maggie asked dubiously. "There are not many who would fit that description."

"Oh, I thought of something else!" the lass said.

"What?" several voices asked in a chorus.

"They said she's tall like her father and her brothers."

"Oh my word," Elizabeth said, lowering into a chair. "'Tis me. Papa was right. The baron plans to steal me and take me home."

"I'll believe it," Maggie said. "Are you sure you know which one would do it?"

Elizabeth's stomach dropped. "It must be the baron, the one from England. He already tried it once. He lied about what my father said and tried to make me go off with him, but he failed."

Maggie glanced over at Will and said, "Barons don't take failure well. If he tried once, he'll try again.

Due to the possible danger to Elizabeth, Maggie and Will offered to retrieve Aunt Jennie, something they should be able to do by late morrow. Their suggestion came as a relief for two reasons—because it allowed Elizabeth to stay by Gil's bedside and continue to awaken him to get him to drink fluid. She'd given him goat's milk and some mead, anything to get him drinking.

Every time she checked under his bandage, it seemed to get worse. Overwrought with worry, she paced and finally stepped out to speak with Magnus. "I must go into town. I need a special ingredient to add to the poultice. What I have is not working, and it doesn't have all the ingredients used in Aunt Brenna's new blend."

"What do you need?"

"'Tis a kind of garlic."

Magnus said, "Then I'll send one of our men for the garlic."

"Nay, I must go," she insisted. "Aunt Jennie said she's only had luck with a certain type. I have to look for it. I cannot explain it. I must look for myself."

"Out of the question, lass. Your sire said you are to stay hidden. Walking through the vendor stalls would not be following his instructions. I will not bend."

"Then send someone to find all the different types they have and bring them to me."

Magnus said, "I'll go. Explain it to me."

She did, describing the garlic to the best of her ability, and Magnus left, leaving two guards inside to stand guard at her door and several outside.

He wasn't gone more than a moment when something else popped into her mind. "Wait, Magnus," she called out, "I thought of something else I need."

She hurried out the door, oblivious to the shouts of the men behind her. While she knew they had been ordered to stop her, she didn't expect them to lay hands on her either.

The guards had always been afraid to touch her. One of the reasons she'd hardly been kissed at her age.

Ignoring them, she hurried out the front of the inn, yelling for Magnus, but he'd already disappeared. Then she saw him. One guard reached for her, but she slipped away and said, "Magnus is right there. I need something else from the market."

Three guards argued behind her, but they allowed her to go after Magnus. He was just a few horse lengths ahead.

It was a relief to leave the sick room for a spell, to be outside in the fresh air and to forget, if only for a moment, that Gil was sick.

"Magnus!" She called out to him, but he didn't stop.

Then he disappeared in the thick crowd. She turned around and motioned to the guards behind her that she was returning, but she never made it. Someone shoved one of the guards, and a fight broke out between the Grant warrior and the stranger. The others went to assist the man, and she stepped out of the way, not wanting to be trampled by the people hollering and shoving each other all around her.

She moved around one stall, surprised to see a child crying not far behind it. Less than a year old, the lad sat in the tall grass sobbing because he was all alone. Elizabeth's heart nearly broke for the boy, so she rushed over to soothe him.

A pair of meaty arms grabbed her around the waist while another set of arms forced a bag over her head. She was tossed in the back of a cart before she was able to scream. The blow to her head made her vision go black.

Her last thoughts were about Gil. He'd never know what happened to her, would he?

CHAPTER THIRTEEN

GIL STOOD AS slowly as he could, just to see if he could manage. A stab of pain tore a light moan from him, but he continued, surprised to find it was feeling much better.

The salve Lizzie had brought must have worked. The fever had come on quickly. He'd been deep in the thick of it when Lizzie arrived. He had a vague memory of her sitting beside his bed. There'd been another woman with her, for part of the time, at least, but he couldn't recall who it had been.

He *did* remember how hard Lizzie had cried against his chest. That was the best motivation he had to get his arse out of bed.

He moved over to the door, opening it with a forced smile.

Except the only people there were Phil and Daw. "Where is everyone?"

"They said they'd be back shortly. They went to get some things from the market," Phil said, throwing an odd look at Daw, who clamped his mouth shut. "You're supposed to eat something when you awaken."

"Aye," Daw said, moving closer. "If you wish to leave earlier, then you have to eat and drink. We're to guard you until Magnus returns. Maggie and Will said they'll be back soon."

The two seemed to be hiding something, but he didn't have the energy to press them, and he had to agree with what they'd said. He had to eat or he'd be useless.

He sat down and sipped from a goblet, realizing he was quite thirsty, and then helped himself to a hunk of bread. His grumbling belly reminded him that he hadn't eaten in days other than Elizabeth lifting his head and forcing liquid down his throat. He'd obliged her only because it was his dear Lizzie.

He wished he could recall more.

He found another goblet and drank down the ale left inside, then made his way to the window, wondering where everyone had gone. Perhaps he had dreamed of Lizzie being by his side. Although he'd seen naught from the window, the door flew open a few moments later, and Jennie Cameron, Will and Maggie, and Thorn hurried inside the chamber. They all looked upset and exhausted.

"What's wrong?" he asked, taking a seat again, already certain something had happened by the identical expressions on their faces.

"Elizabeth has gone missing," Maggie said.

Gil bolted off his chair…nay, he only tried. The pain stopped him from moving far.

"Hellfire," he hissed, grabbing his wound. "I thought 'twas better."

"Come inside the bed chamber, and I'll change the dressing." Jennie Grant was not one to argue with, he guessed, but she didn't understand how he felt about Elizabeth either.

"Nay, I must go after Elizabeth."

"Sit down," she insisted. "I've come this far, and I'll do my part for Elizabeth. You'll not get past me, you see. I have fifty guards outside."

He stared at Jennie Cameron, youngest sister to Alexander Grant, and decided he wouldn't argue with her any more than he would her brother. Not wanting to appear ungrateful, he nodded and said, "My apologies. I'd appreciate you taking a look and helping if you can. 'Tis not healing quickly at all."

Maggie crossed her arms and said, "Good idea, Gil, because you'll not waste your chance to be treated by one of the finest healers in all the land. Will and I would have held you down if you'd refused. Clearly, you're upset about Elizabeth, but you'll not get verra far if you don't heal." She pointed to the chamber, so Gil moved inside, still favoring his uninjured side. "I'll send Will out to search for more clues about her disappearance. Everyone else is already out there looking."

"Is it your leg or your hip?" Jennie asked, while Maggie spoke with Will.

"Both," he replied, not wishing to stay back, but knowing Maggie was right. He'd be more valuable if he were healed. He didn't doubt he needed a skilled healer, and Jennie Cameron had a reputation known throughout the land. "It grazed my hip, but the deepest cut is in the top part of my thigh. 'Tis where it festered the most." He lifted his plaid, careful to maintain his dignity.

"That must have been quite a fever," Jennie said. "I'll need to give you a potion and more poultice. But first I'll need to scrub it out. I won't like doing so because 'twill hurt a bit."

"Do what you must, as fast as you can, so I can go after her. Please tell me exactly what happened."

"I wasn't here, mind you, but I heard what Magnus discussed with the guards. He was headed to market for more supplies. Elizabeth thought of something else she needed and chased after him, but she never caught him. She turned back toward the inn, only a short distance away, when a scuffle broke out between two of the Grant guards and three strangers, which drew the other guards' attention. When they turned around, Elizabeth was gone. They have no idea how they managed to get her away without anyone seeing anything."

Maggie, who'd slipped into the room in time to hear the end, added, "Magnus never saw her behind him, so he kept moving through the stalls. The only other information I could glean from the vendors close to the inn was they saw a cart leave the area. They noticed because carts aren't allowed there. Said it was moving quickly."

"So they knocked her out and put her in the cart. Any information on the men who drove the cart? English, Scottish?"

"Nay, no one could identify them."

He growled in frustration. "As soon as I can get something to eat, I'm leaving."

"I understand," Jenny said. "I'm going to reinforce your stitches, so I think they'll hold. I'll send some salve with you in addition to what you put on the wound. I would recommend you go straight to Grant land. It will hurt, but I know many stubborn men, and I can tell whatever I say will not stop you. I also know we need to tell my brother as soon as possible. Alex will tear the

Highlands apart looking for his daughter."

Gil's expression firmed. "As will I."

Elizabeth awakened inside a lavish chamber. She lay on a large bed, her mantle and boots arranged next to the door where a man stood guard. She sat up and stared at him. "Where am I?"

He didn't answer but opened the door and whistled. A few moments later, a woman in a plain dress entered the chamber. "I'll have a bath brought up for you, my lady, along with a platter of fruit and cheese. Can I get you anything else?"

"No need for those items since I plan on taking my leave. I'll put my boots and mantle on, and be on my way."

The woman cleared her throat and stared at the floor. "You'll not be leaving, my lady. He'd never allow it."

"He, who? Who brought me here?"

"I'm not allowed to say," the woman said nervously, "but I'll go get your food." She started to turn around, then glanced back at her worriedly. "There are five guards in the passageway and along the staircase with orders to keep you inside."

"Who is it? I wish to talk to the bastard." Ignoring the pounding in her head, she settled her hands on her hips.

"I'll tell him you are awake, and I'm sure he'll come to see you soon, but I can say naught about this place. Please forgive me." Before leaving the room, she glanced back one final time. "My name if Forsy should you need me." Then she did a small curtsy and left.

The guard at the door gave her a wide grin. "I'm allowed to force you back onto the bed if you become difficult, lass. I can tie you there, too." The grin he wore made her shudder. She chose to wait.

"Never mind. You'll pay the price when my sire and my brothers find out about this." She stood up and leaned against the bed post. "You do know who my sire is, do you not?"

"Your sire is an old man."

"An old man with three large sons, one taller and broader than he is. Four of the finest swordsmen in the land."

"They aren't much trouble when they don't know where you are, are they? By the time they get here, it'll be too late. The master will have to teach you a thing or two, but I hope someday you'll become a fine biddable woman for him. He's in need of a mistress to tend to all of his needs." Then the man belted out a wicked laugh that made no mystery of his thoughts. "He'll not be content until he has three sons. You'll need to lie back and do what a woman was made for."

Elizabeth strode over and stood in front of him, crossing her arms. "In my clan, a woman holds more value than a brood mare. My aunt used to spy for the Crown. And she'll pin you to the wall by your bollocks."

The man was enjoying their banter, she could tell, because he of course believed himself to be the smarter of the two of them.

"I've heard those tales and don't believe any of them." The glint in his eyes told her he thought all the tales were lies.

"You could ask Bearchun, if he'd lived to tell the tale. He was stuck to the tree for a long time while the buzzards pecked at his bollocks."

"You've got a crude mouth for a lass. Act like a lady, because you'll have little choice once you're married." He moved back toward the door, giving her his back.

"I'll not marry your master. My family will save me."

And yet, her mind didn't muster an image of her father storming in, but rather Gil.

He would, she knew that, if he weren't lying in bed ill with fever.

"Bride stealing has been allowed for years. Once you stand in front of the priest, there's nothing your clan can do to stop it." He turned around to wink at her.

"You'll never get me to say aye and I have to."

"Believe what you'd like. We'll see who's right," he called out over his shoulder as he sauntered out of the room.

The door closed behind him, and she couldn't stop herself from pacing. It was a lovely chamber, so the person who owned it had to be quite wealthy. The bed had the most lovely curtains, tied back with ropes. The thick covering on the floor had a woven design of muted blue and gold thread, unlike anything she'd ever seen. It was lovely to look at and much nicer on the feet than rushes. The bed itself was piled with pillows and furs, the fine linens something she hadn't felt before.

Forsy appeared Scottish, yet the guard spoke like an Englishman.

It had to be the baron. The English would have such possessions before anyone in the Highlands, and they would have Scots and English working for them. The chamber also featured multiple chests, so she spent the next several minutes searching them. There were more linens, towels, furs, and night rails, but nothing that could be used as a weapon.

"Drat," she whispered. The door opened and a group of lads entered carrying the tub, followed by other lads carrying basins of steaming water.

But the last piece they brought in was the most important—a partition she could hide behind. Part of her wanted to reject the offer on principle, but she felt as dirty as a dog rolling in the mud, and the steaming water was too tempting to pass up. After the lads left, she disrobed and stepped into it.

Forsy came inside and arranged the linens and sweet-smelling soaps for her. "Would you like any assistance, my lady?"

"Nay, I'll be fine. I'd appreciate it if you'd guard the door for me. I'd like some privacy."

Forsy nodded and settled on a stool by the door.

Steeping in the warm water, Elizabeth's mind went right back to Gil. Had Aunt Jennie made it to his side? How she prayed she had.

What a mess she'd made of everything. Had they been open about their relationship, this never would have happened. Her parents wouldn't have made it known she needed a suitor, and Gil wouldn't have gone to Edinburgh. No one would have given any thought to taking her as a bride.

Regrets…so many regrets.

CHAPTER FOURTEEN

THE GROUP LEFT shortly thereafter, Gil hurrying them along. Thorn, Daw, Phil, Will and Maggie traveled with him, and Magnus and his men had stayed behind in Edinburgh in the hopes of finding more evidence left by the kidnappers.

Jennie had created a large padding around Gil's wound to protect it and keep the yellow pus at bay, and although it pained him, he was able to keep pace with the others.

Before they arrived on Cameron land, she said, "Take care of your wound, Gil. I know you are pressed to do other things, but you have to survive for Elizabeth. She didn't come all the way to Edinburgh to see you die. I know my niece well enough to know that you have her heart, based on what I've heard, so please guard it well."

"Have you talked with her, Jennie?" He had no idea how she could have guessed about their relationship. They'd hidden everything so well. Or so they had thought.

"I don't need to. If she traveled to Edinburgh without her parents or any of her brothers, she's in love with you. Elizabeth doesn't like to leave her family. Especially her parents."

"'Struth. Will I ever convince her she can leave them?" If Jennie knew they were together, there was no reason for him not to ask such a private question. He wanted an opinion from an outside observer. But she needed to know he was in earnest. "I love her verra much and hope to make her my wife someday."

"She'll leave them for the right person," she said, studying him. "Living at Castle Curanta would suit both of you. From what I've heard, you are both magical with the wee bairns."

That surprised him, that Jennie would know about the work

they did.

"Don't look shocked. Instead imagine how much good the two of you could do if you didn't hide all you do—and your interest in each other. Think on it, and please act on it. I'd like to see my brother give Elizabeth away to a good man."

She took leave of them at the juncture leading to Cameron land, wishing them luck in their journey. Jennie had given him much to think about. She'd also given him everything he needed to care for his wound, but right now, he wasn't concerned about it. He needed to find Elizabeth.

They took a short break in a clearing to discuss their plans and eat some of the oatcakes from their packs.

"How much farther?" Daw asked.

Will said, "Do you see those mountains? We're going to where the tops touch the sky, where you can look down and see nothing but greenery, a beauty unlike you've ever seen before."

"Truly? That nice?" Phil asked.

"Nicer than you think," Maggie said. "Ah, Will's falcons have arrived." She whistled, and two birds circled closer to them, one bird larger than the other.

"Are those the wild falcons? Will they peck out my eyes if Will tells them to?" Phil asked, hiding behind Gil a bit as they all stared overhead.

Will let out another whistle and then held his arm out. The larger falcon came down slowly and landed on his arm. Will grabbed something from his pocket and fed it to the bird.

"Will it attack me?" Daw asked as the bird studied him.

"Nay, she's just checking you over. Wants to see who you are. She'll not bother you unless you come after me."

Gil had to laugh, the two bairns were enamored of the birds, yet still a wee bit afraid of them. He recalled feeling the same way the first time he'd seen the falcons up close. The bird tipped its head back and forth, looking at the group. Maggie held her arm up, and the smaller bird lighted on her thick sleeve, fanning its wings wide open as it did so.

"They're pretty," Phil said.

Will moved his arm up, and the great bird took to flight, Maggie's bird following. "We have to move on."

They'd planned to go to Grant Castle first, but Gil found himself restless, eager to see Loki and Kenzie and Thorn. Eager to find Elizabeth the best way he knew how—with the men he trusted most.

"I know I should be the one to talk with Alex because my relationship with Elizabeth has caused this mess," he said, scratching the back of his head, "but I'd like to go straight to Loki. We've always strategized well together. We'll make a plan, stop on Grant land to see if they've learned anything, and move on from there."

Will nodded. "Maggie and I will go to Grant land and face Alex and the lairds. I have a message for Jake from Magnus. He definitely considers this his fault, and he won't rest until she's found."

Maggie shook her head slightly, her smile mirthful. "They'd have caught up with us on the trail back home if not in Edinburgh. Beautiful brides are a sign of power in the Highlands. Whoever's after her would not have backed down so easily."

Will said, "In my opinion, waiting until she was three and twenty to look for suitors fueled it. Her brothers expected trouble."

"And the state of unrest after the king's death has not helped the situation," Maggie added. "King Edward thinks he can pull the Grants and Ramsays to heel to his every whim, and Alex still has the reputation as the most powerful man in the Highlands. Edward wants to see how far he can push them. He'll find 'tis not far. Alex doesn't realize how beneficial it was for him to have three sons. It makes for a powerful quartet."

Will glanced at her and said, "I'm quite sure he is perfectly aware of it. His skill as a strategist was shown when they put Jamie and Jake in power at such a young age. He's training the three of them well."

"Agreed," Maggie said. "That move was the sign of a brilliant mind. That, and keeping them all on his land instead of granting them lairdships and spreading their power. Their numbers are phenomenal. I wonder if he can even count all of the Grant warriors."

Thorn laughed, "Jamie can. He's the number person. And so is Kyla."

"You go see Loki, Gil. We'll tend to Uncle Alex," Maggie suggested. "We'll help them prepare a group to travel with you. You'll need some Grant warriors if the baron took her, and having one of the Grant lairds along will only improve your chances. You should work together."

"I agree with your plan, and you have my eternal gratitude for helping me through this. We have to find Lizzie."

Maggie smiled at him. "It pleases me verra much to see that Elizabeth has found someone, Gil. I know you'll treat her well."

"I love her with all my heart. I just need to find her, see she is hale, then I'll convince her we belong together." He rubbed his hand across the roughness of his beard. It felt strange to admit the truth in front of an audience, but it was also freeing.

"You haven't yet?" she asked, surprised. "She came all the way to Edinburgh for you."

"We're happy together, but we hadn't planned on rushing into marriage. Our agreement was to wait a while longer, though no more than a year. I feel differently now. I'd do anything to have her at Castle Curanta or Grant Castle." They slowed their horses through the ravine leading into Grant land.

"Easy to remedy. You'll get your opportunity soon."

"If her father approves. I feared he wouldn't accept me, and I'll admit I'm even more worried now." He glanced at Maggie, feeling the fear rake his insides as keenly as if it were a sword. He ached with the need just to see her, hear her voice. Anything to know she was hale. "He'll probably never approve of our marriage after this catastrophe."

"'Tis not over yet. Do not worry about something that hasn't happened. My sister is a seer, though she doesn't tell many about the sights she has these days. Do you know what she told me before I left Ramsay land?"

"I have no idea," Gil said, interested despite himself.

"She told me that Elizabeth was about to become extremely happy. We didn't even know we were going to *see* Elizabeth."

Gil nearly snorted with derision. "Whatever she saw was completely wrong."

"Was it? What if this situation forces the two of you into the relationship you should have had long ago? I'm going to guess that if the two of you get through this together, both healed and unhurt, there will be a wedding soon. And if so, I think Elizabeth will be overflowing with happiness." She winked at him. "'Tis how I'm going to view this situation. 'Twill definitely help when we speak with Alex and her brothers."

"I can only pray you are correct. I hope to see you soon, after we form our patrol at Castle Curanta."

Once they reached the juncture leading to Grant land, Gil said, "Godspeed to you," and Thorn added, "I'll make sure we get him home safely."

"Be aware you will probably run into different Grant patrols on your way back," Will said. "Alex will not wait to search all of the Highlands, and he has the manpower to do it."

The groups parted ways, and as he and Thorn rode toward Castle Curanta, Gil found himself thinking about the conversation he was about to have with his laird. He finally felt ready to share the truth. He might have failed on this journey to Edinburgh, but he'd realized something.

He valued having Lizzie in his life more than he cared about impressing her sire. In his ideal world, the two could coexist, but he'd sacrifice anything, including his own life, for Lizzie.

He had to find her before it was too late.

Dizzy from fatigue, he arrived at the gates to Castle Curanta along with Thorn, Phillipa, Daw, and the rest of the guards. Loki came out to greet the visitor, his expression registering surprise when he saw their faces.

"You were ordered to stay at least a sennight. Why did you come back too soon?"

"Lizzie's been kidnapped."

"Rat bastards," Loki mumbled. "And you look like hell." That came out in more of a yell.

"He's barely allowed us to stop," Thorn said.

"I must tell you all," Gil said. Then he paused, his hand going to his sore leg, and a deep sigh escaped his lips.

Loki gave directions to the stable lads. "Thorn will explain, Daw and Phillipa will tell me anything he forgets. You are to get yourself into a chair, not a stool, in the keep and find yourself something to eat."

Gil couldn't argue because food and a seat did sound appealing. Much as he wished to race after Lizzie without delay, he was useless, so he had to pray Magnus had managed to locate her. At the moment, he needed to restore his strength and regroup.

They made their way into the keep, Herry there to greet them. "You do not look well, Master Gil," Herry said with an expression of fear and worry.

"Sit down, Gil," Bella said, studying him with concern. "I'll get my healing bag."

"No need," Gil said. "Jennie Grant restitched it after the healer from Edinburgh botched the job. She also rebandaged it and gave me salve to use."

Bella turned to Loki. "Feed him something first, then bring him to my healing chamber. I'll need to take a look at his wound. And don't listen to him, Loki. He needs to have it cleaned and bandaged again."

Loki nodded, a glance passing between the husband and wife that he didn't understand.

"What did that mean?" he asked.

"It means you need to heal some before you can go chasing after Elizabeth," Loki said bluntly. "We all know you're going to be stubborn about it, and Bella expects me to stop you. So why are you so driven?" Turning to Thorn, he asked, "Why did Elizabeth even go there? We met up with them on our way home, but I never heard her reasons for leaving Clan Grant. I'm doing my best to patiently wait for an explanation, but you and I both know how Alex Grant will react to his wee blonde lassie going missing. I don't care how old she is. His bellow will be heard all the way to the royal burgh." He ran his hand through his long locks as he paced in front of the hearth. "The only thing that will prevent him from coming in this direction will be Elizabeth. He'll go for her first, then come after us."

Gil sat down while Thorn filled Loki in on everything. Almost everything. He had much to tell Loki too, but he wanted privacy. There was a confession to be made, and he didn't want an audience to hear it.

He listened carefully to see if Thorn missed any details, but he did a fine job relaying the pertinent information. Herry had pulled Phillipa and Daw aside and was busy showing them around the keep. He couldn't help but smile when Herry said, "You should see where we get to sleep! And the food is the best. I've been helping in the stables because they have so many horses."

"Archery," Phil said. "Where do they practice archery?"

"I'll show you," Herry said, enjoying being the source of information for the other two.

Once they were out of hearing, Loki said, "Now I'll hear the real reason Elizabeth was in Edinburgh. Thorn's claim that she simply wished to help doesn't quite work for me." His piercing gaze told Gil he wasn't going to hide anything from him, not that he had a mind to anymore. But he would still prefer not to discuss the situation so publicly.

"Lizzie and I…"

"Lizzie? She allows you to call her Lizzie? She doesn't even allow the wee bairns to call her that."

"Aye, she allows me to call her Lizzie, but only when we're alone." He leaned over and whispered the last part. "We have been seeing each other…"

Loki held his hand up. "I think I can guess the rest, so save your breath until we're in the healing chamber. Eat first, then we'll see Bella and you can tell us both."

Gil sighed and gave him a nod, dropping his gaze. He had a brief respite to decide exactly what he would say. After two meat pies and one ale, Loki clasped his shoulder, "Into the healing chamber with you. Thorn can get something to eat while Bella takes care of you."

Gil stood, only swaying a bit as Loki led him away, but it struck him that part of his problem was fatigue. Perhaps he could take a quick nap while Bella fixed him up. She greeted them in the healing chamber, then said, "Come right over here, Gil. Do you have that salve Jennie sent with you? I'm sure 'tis most excellent, and another dab will serve you well."

Gil handed the salve to Bella and settled on the pallet, uncovering the wound so she could work on it. "My, but Jennie did some fine stitching over the bad ones. Whoever did it first made a right mess of it."

"We did what we had to, Bella," Loki said, "it was a healer from the area."

She applied the salve, then finished rebandaging the wound. Gil sat up, suddenly anxious, and glanced from Loki to Bella. He trusted her as much as he did Loki though, and suddenly he couldn't wait to speak. "Loki, I must speak the truth to you," he blurted out, "so please listen. I'm in love with Lizzie, and we have been seeing each other in secret for about seven moons. I love her, but she didn't wish to leave her family and I wanted to continue to work with the bairns." He shook his head. "The reasons aren't important at the moment, just know we decided to wait before letting everyone know of our relationship. So we kept it a secret from all. But now I'm ready to tell you that losing her isn't worth it. I have to find her. I'm sorry if it means I'll be going to Grant Castle, but I'm going no farther than that. I should have stayed away from Edinburgh. It's all my fault, and I have to find her. I have to. Please help me."

There. The truth was out. Well, almost all of it. But Loki knew the important parts of everything that had transpired.

Loki and Bella exchanged a look, then he said, "Hell, Gil. I'm not surprised. We knew you had your eye on someone, but you kept a good secret."

"So you'll help me?"

"Aye, once you admit the true reason you kept this all hidden."

"What?" he asked, baffled.

"Gil, everyone can guess your reasons for keeping everything secret," Bella said kindly. "You didn't want everyone to know, but I would guess it was just a certain few you worried about. Mayhap Elizabeth has the same fear."

"What fear?"

Loki chortled. "Are you going to try to deny it? The true reason you both kept it secret was because you were afraid to ask Alex Grant for his daughter's hand in marriage."

"What. Nay." But shite, he had a point. Hadn't Elizabeth told him, again and again, he did not have to prove himself to her sire?

"Nay?" Bella said. "I don't know a man who wouldn't be afraid to pursue Alex's youngest. I mean, there is Maeve, but she hasn't been with them since birth. Elizabeth has been their wee bairn for a long time, wrapped around his chest for moons. Alex doesn't want her married."

"And neither does Maddie," Loki said. "So no one will be surprised to hear you've hidden it from them."

"'Struth? You think they are aware of it?"

"Och, I didn't say that," Loki said with a grin. "He doesn't think he's coddling her. He thinks Maddie coddles her."

"And Maddie thinks Alex coddles her too much," Bella finished. "Neither of them will want to lose her. You've got a challenge when the time comes to ask for her hand in marriage. But if anyone can do it, you can, Gil. I believe in you."

Gil looked from one to the other, unable to take in all he just heard.

Loki asked, "How did Elizabeth end up in Edinburgh? Did Alex allow it?"

Gil scratched his head and replied, "She heard about my injury and showed up with Magnus and some other Grant guards. I'm sure she confessed our relationship to one of her brothers and they allowed it. Whether Alex knows yet, I don't know."

"Connor would have allowed it in an instant. He should have gone with her. We have to tell Alex. He'll tear the Highlands apart looking for her."

Gil shook his head.

Bella asked, "What is it, Gil?"

"I should never have gone. My gut has always told me that I should never return to Edinburgh. I should have listened."

Loki let out a deep sigh, shaking his light brown hair. "'Tis too late to look back. We look forward, Gil. Tell me again who is where."

"Magnus is still patrolling Edinburgh with his guards, looking for information that might lead us to her. We met up with Maggie and Will. They have gone off to tell Alex and the lairds. I have to find her. I have to go after her. I love her and wish to make her my wife."

Loki patted his shoulder. "I won't let you go for an hour, so you may as well close your eyes for a wee bit. I think you need it."

He couldn't argue that. With a sigh, he laid his head down

and nearly fell asleep, but then said, "You'll awaken me after one hour?"

"Aye," a voice called out, though he didn't know which one.

He couldn't answer because he fell asleep before the word ended.

CHAPTER FIFTEEN

ELIZABETH CLIMBED OUT of the tub and dressed in the night rail laid out for her by Forsy. She stood on the other side of the large bed while the lads returned and moved the tub. Once they were done, she turned to Forsy. "Will your master see me now?"

"Nay, he said he'd allow you the night's rest. I'll bring you the dress you're to wear for the wedding early morn. Is there anything else I can do for you, my lady? If not, I'll leave you to your rest. Dark is nigh upon us, and I've had a long day."

She smiled at Forsy and gave her permission to leave, having no more need for her. The maid lit a few candles in the sconces before she left, offering one last comment. "I'll see you on the morrow, my lady. Sleep well."

Elizabeth found it hard to dislike her, but there was no way in hell she would be here on the morrow. She hurried over to the window and pulled the fur back, peering out through the slats in the shutters.

A sigh of relief gusted out of her. Her window was at the back of the keep and only on the second floor. She could easily tie something to the bed and shimmy out of the window. Her gaze searched the curtain wall for a door, finally finding one in the back corner.

She'd be escaping soon, but she'd have to wait until dark.

She busied herself with getting the bed ready, loosening the curtains around it so it was covered, arranging the pillows so it looked like someone was asleep beneath the covers, then she glanced at what she'd tossed onto the floor—the ropes that had held the curtains back.

The ropes. There were four of them, made of strong material. Could she tie them together and climb out the window? She'd thought to use some linens, but the ropes would definitely be stronger.

She made quick work of it, looping and tying the ropes easily. Her sire had taught her rope skills long ago, for she'd never had an interest in archery or swordplay. They'd started when she was but five summers. She'd often wondered why her sire had chosen to teach her, until it struck her that it was because of her interest in horses. She was often in the stables, and one of her favorite past times was to make sleek decorations for her mare, tying her mane into fancy woven patterns, using fine rope to loop the strands together.

She'd never expected the skill to prove so invaluable. "My thanks to you, Papa," she whispered, as if he were standing nearby.

Once she finished, she set the ropes in front of the window and sat down, knowing she had to wait a wee bit longer before escaping. Dusk had fallen and the sounds of night were dissipating but not enough. She waited until all was quiet outside her door, then changed back into her clothing, donning the trews she always wore under her gown when traveling. Her gown wasn't in the best shape, but she had to wear something, and it would not be the dress her captor planned to marry her in.

She wouldn't leave until all was quiet outside.

Fighting the tears that threatened to come, she forced herself to think on happy things. Her mind landed on Gil, on their first night of lovemaking. He'd been so kind, so gentle, and while she'd known a little about the act from her sister, she hadn't expected it to be so wonderful. Hearing her name on his lips as he gave over to his climax, being held like she was a fragile piece of glass, lying with their bodies intertwined afterward—it was all nearly as sweet as the peak of their joining. Gil had taught her about true love, about how it felt to put someone else's needs ahead of her own.

She'd never stop loving him.

But it was too painful to think of Gil, who might still be wracked with fever, so she pushed the memory aside. The one that popped up in its place made her smile.

Once, when she was a wee lassie, her mother had asked Cook to try a new recipe for a lamb meat pie. Her father was set in his ways sometimes, averse to change, so her mother had brought her to the kitchens and asked her to stir the gravy so she could say Elizabeth had helped make it. Elizabeth, being quite young at the time, had believed it to be partly her creation. They'd even helped Cook stuff the pies before she baked them. Elizabeth still remembered how excited she'd been as they came out of the oven. She'd run out of the kitchens and straight to the hearth with a platter, eager for her father to try her new treat. Her mother had followed, not saying a word, but clearly complicit in the endeavor.

He'd peered at the platter, then glanced up at her mother and said, "You changed my favorite meat pie, Maddie? Why?"

"Alex, your daughter helped us make them, and somehow they came out different. Give it a try."

He'd moved over to the mantel of the hearth, crossing his arms in front of him. "Mayhap I'm no longer hungry."

Elizabeth had thought he was unhappy with her, and her lip had started to quiver, her face scrunching up before she burst into tears. One look at her had her father grabbing the meat pie, and he ate nearly the entire pastry in one bite.

Her sobs had stopped, but the tears continued to roll down her cheeks until her father said, "Maddie, 'tis the best meat pie I've ever eaten."

Then he'd swung Elizabeth up into his arms and kissed her cheek. "Dry your tears, wee one. 'Tis most delicious."

Many years had passed before Elizabeth had caught on to the way people used her sire's affection for her to get him to try something new. It made her even fonder of him. More determined to make him proud by escaping the bastard who'd thought he could kidnap a Grant.

Standing, she donned her mantle and moved over to the window. She hooked the fur and opened the shutter, peeking out to see if the back was empty. Pleased to see no one within view, she carefully tested the rope one more time, tied it to a bedpost, and slowly lowered it from the window. Climbing with her mantle on would not be easy, especially in a gown, so she dropped it to the ground outside the window before tying her gown up to her waist and shimmying down the rope. Luckily, she was wearing trews, something she often did before a long ride.

It proved more difficult than she'd expected, her arms nearly giving out from the strain, but she held firm until she dropped to the bottom. Scooping up her mantle, she quickly arranged it over her shoulders and headed to the door in the corner of the curtain wall. All was quiet and she crept out easily.

Once she closed the outside door behind her, she breathed a sigh of relief because she was free.

The only problem was she had no horse and no idea which way to go. But she would trudge along as quickly as she could, praying to find someone, anyone, who might help her. Her father and Loki would have patrols out everywhere, but would they have made it to England already? She had to guess her captor was the baron, since he was the one who'd attempted to use trickery to try to get her away from her sire.

Who else could it be?

She found a path and followed it, grateful to the full moon and the cloudless night for giving her some guidance. After she ran a short distance, her hair started whipping around in her face so she used her tie to pull it back like a man might.

Once her hair was tied at her crown, she found a steady pace, something she knew was paramount for escaping her captor.

Whoever the bastard was.

She ran for hours, her legs tiring and cramping, chiding herself for forgetting the most basic items. Why hadn't she brought along a hunk of cheese or bread? Her hair still caught in brambles, scratching her face multiple times, she tripped in a hole and turned her ankle, but still she didn't stop.

She vowed to continue on because she'd never marry the bastard who'd captured her, whoever he was.

Her thoughts turned back to Gil, the man she'd agreed to marry. The man she wished to spend the rest of her life with. Had he made it back home? Was he worried for her?

Hours passed, and she felt no closer to Grant land then when she left. Dying of thirst, she decided the time had come to pay attention to her surroundings. She slowed to a walk and listened as the birds woke up, chirping loudly, the squirrels now chattering and searching for nuts. The sound of water trickling wasn't far away. Following it, she located a small burn, giggling at the rippling of the water when it hit the rocks. She tipped her head sideways to lap some up, the taste more wonderful than she could have imagined.

When she finally felt she'd had enough, she got to her feet, only to immediately freeze in her tracks. The earth rumbled under her feet.

Horses. Horses were headed in her direction, but would it be friends or enemies?

She had to make a decision.

CHAPTER SIXTEEN

ALEX WOULDN'T REST until his dearest Elizabeth had returned. His gut told him he'd made a huge mistake allowing her to travel to Edinburgh, but they'd sent her with Magnus and a powerful group of guards. He'd believed there was no reason to worry.

Visitors came to the gate unexpectedly, and the sound of their approach caused his gut to roil a bit more. He recognized their voices even from his perch in the parapets. Maggie and Will, while very dear to him, usually were not the bearers of good news. Spies for the Scottish Crown, their work had become more hazardous after King Alexander III had snapped his neck in a fall off his horse.

His daughter did not appear to be among them. Usually her golden hair would be easy to spot, but the only lass he saw from his vantage point was Maggie. He had to get to the gates because there would be a definite reason those two had come at such a time.

His breath caught in his chest as he descended the steps, cut through the great hall, and made his way to the gate with Connor and Jake, whom he'd caught up with in the courtyard.

None of the three had spoken as they fell into line with one another. Alex didn't need to ask to know they shared his concern—he could tell by looking at their faces.

"Welcome, Will, Maggie," Jake said. "We'll take care of your horses if you'll join us inside for a bite to eat." He motioned for two lads to take their horses to the stables. "Brush them down and feed them well, lads."

Alex didn't speak until the two were dismounted and the lads had left them. Finally, he said, "'Tis Elizabeth, is it not?"

Maggie searched the area for prying ears before she answered, "Aye. She was kidnapped not far from the inn in Edinburgh. She'd followed Magnus out to ask him to get something else for her at the market. She wasn't far from the inn when a scuffle broke out, drawing everyone's attention, and someone snatched her. It happened in the space of a few moments. Magnus and your guards are still out searching."

"Give my sons the details inside, and I'll join you shortly," Alex said. "Answer me this first. How is Gil?"

"We traveled back with him. His wound was severe and he fought the fever, but your sister, Jennie, helped him. He went straight to Loki for reinforcements. They'll be on the road by morning."

"My thanks to you for coming to advise us of the situation so quickly. We'll have search teams out shortly. I will lead one of them." He nodded to the group and found his horse, mounting in one fluid move and taking off into the distance. He paused just long enough to look back at Connor and say, "Tell your mother I'll return shortly."

Will had made his way straight to Jamie and looked to be rapidly updating his son on the situation. They didn't need him.

He knew it might upset Maddie, but she knew him better than anyone. It wouldn't surprise her that he'd needed to visit the private place he'd created for moments when he needed to be alone. He'd built it on an overlook so he could see anyone climbing the mountain to enter his land. Other than that, it had been chosen for its abundance of pines. This was the one place where he allowed himself to lose all control and get rid of his rage. Maddie wasn't allowed, only his sons.

Never had he needed it more.

A bastard had stolen his dearest Elizabeth, had dared to steal her in the middle of Edinburgh. Over the years, he'd learned to control his temper, but this…*this*…this was too much.

When he reached the spot, he jumped off his horse and found the perfect pine tree. Unsheathing his sword, he lifted it over his head and brought it down hard on the first branch, slicing it cleanly off. He continued on and on until there was little left of the tree. His breath ragged, he wiped the sweat from his brow and sat on a tree stump for a few moments, though he knew not how long. If he didn't get rid of his rage here, he'd take it out on others. He'd tie up anyone he suspected of complicity in the kidnapping and beat them until they talked.

But that was wrong and he knew it. Learning to control his temper was one of the hardest things he'd ever done, but he'd done it for Maddie, because he could see how much his rage frightened her. Coming out here alone allowed him to go back home with a cooler head, to achieve the right frame of mind to strategize and plan. Otherwise, his emotions ruled his actions.

The only son who seemed to have the same temperament was Jake. They'd come out here together before, and indeed, it appeared Jake had also come out on his own. Alex had felled and struck many trees, but not all the ones showing slices in their bark.

His breathing now under control, he got up and went after another tree, imagining that the bark was the baron who'd dared to touch his daughter. *His bairn.*

His Elizabeth!

After a time, he heard a horse approaching, so he stopped his swings and moved over to the tree stump that overlooked a gorge, a lovely view of the Highlands in the distance. It was Connor, which wasn't unexpected. Maddie usually sent one of their sons out to check on him.

The surprise came when Connor arrived, because he wasn't alone. His young daughter Dyna, her white hair as bright as the sun, sat in front of him, her expression serious.

"What is it?" Alex shouted.

Connor took Dyna's hand and they strode over to him. "You are finished and feel better?" he asked.

"Aye," Alex answered, wiping his sweaty face with the sleeve of his tunic. "Why is she here?" Connor knew the rules as well as any of them. He didn't wish for any lasses to venture near this place. His anger was not something that made him proud. He would only approve of Dyna's presence if there were special circumstances.

Of course, Dyna *was* special. She had an uncanny way of knowing things.

"Go ahead and tell Grandpapa," Connor said with a nod.

As bold as a woman of thirty years, she stared at Alex, eyes boring into him, and said, "The lads are here watching."

"What?" Alex asked, his gaze searching the area. "I don't see them. How do you know this, lass? Did they tell you they were coming?"

"Nay," she said, pursing her lips. "I see them here." She pointed to her forehead. "And they're hiding in the trees. They followed you."

Her words sent a tingle down his spine. He didn't doubt her.

"Where, Dyna?" Connor asked.

She pointed to an area where the trees were thicker. "In there."

"Alasdair, Alick, and Elshander," Alex shouted. "You have until I count to three to show yourselves. One…two…"

Els ran out yelling, "Dyna, why do you tattle so?" His cousins followed him out, shamefaced.

Alex pointed to the spot in front of him. "All three of you there. Explain yourselves."

Alick looked to Els, then they both looked to Alasdair, the one who usually spoke for the three of them.

"We heard that Aunt Elizabeth was taken and we want to help get her back," Alasdair said, the words coming so quickly it was difficult to understand him. "We can help by hiding and watching like we did here, then we can come and get you, Grandpapa, or Uncle Connor. We must help! We wanted to watch you practice so we could get better and…"

Alex held his hand up to stop the lad's rambling. "How did you get here? Where are your horses?"

"We ran," Alick answered. The look of determination on their faces made an impression on him. Not for the first time, he had the premonition that these three lads, born on the same day, at the same time, were special. Dyna was too, and when their time came, the four would do something great.

"Grandpapa," Connor said, his tone deadly serious, "should we have them move that big pile of dirt behind the keep?"

Alex had to smirk at that. The three lads' eyes were larger than the biggest chestnuts he'd ever seen. The day he'd punished Jake and Jamie by forcing them to move rocks from one spot to another for hours was one of the clan's favorite tales. The fear it invoked in the three faces nearly made him laugh, but he held it in. The lads were young and trying their best to do what was right.

"Nay, I think not. But they will ride back because I have no time to watch over their walk. Lads, I appreciate your spirit, but we'll not need your help this time." He ruffled the closest mop of hair, which happened to be Elshander's golden locks, a mess of curls at present. "Alasdair with Uncle Connor, Alick and Els with me. Mount up."

"Are you sure you're finished, Papa?

"Aye, I'm done." They made their way back to the horses and the three lads continued rambling, one to Dyna, the other two to Connor.

"You should have seen Grandpapa swing at that one tree, he was faster than anyone and the ground shook and the branches fell down and then the tree fell over."

"You're all lucky you weren't hurt," Connor said.

Once they headed back, Alex pulled his horse abreast of Connor's. "When do we leave?"

"Within the hour. Jake is gathering the groups now. Three separate patrols. One with you, one with me, one with him. Jamie is to stay at the keep. Maggie and Will ride with me."

"Sounds like a good plan. You lads and lass will stay back, understood?"

A chorus answered them, some louder than others, "Aye, Grandpapa."

"Alasdair, I'll have your word as a Highlander," Alex said. As Jake's son, he was a bit more headstrong than the others.

He heard the lad mutter under his breath, "Drat." Then clearly said, "Aye, Grandpapa. You have my word I will stay back."

"You three are charged with making sure no one attacks our castle," Alex continued. "This could be a ruse to get our warriors away so someone can overtake our keep. Under no circumstances are you to leave, or you will make our castle vulnerable to attack. I think it best to watch from the parapets." He knew that much would gain favor with the lads. They enjoyed going up there whenever patrols left. "Dyna, your job is to keep an eye on them."

Dyna just smiled, a smug look on her face. The lass was full of personality and knew more than most adults.

He hoped she couldn't read what was in his mind.

CHAPTER SEVENTEEN

ELIZABETH HAD ONE desperate problem, she was exhausted after running through the night. Her clothes were in ruin, her face and hands bleeding from the brush and brambles she'd come through in the dark, and while she'd quenched her thirst, the hunger was starting to overtake her thinking.

She forced herself to peer onto the main path to see who'd found her. A voice rang out in the dark. "Over there! I see her."

"We'll get the bitch."

Ten horses headed in her direction. She was quite sure no one from her clan would had called her a bitch. It had to be her captors, so she tried to run back into the forest, but two men dismounted and chased after her, one meaty arm grabbing her from behind while another came at her from the side. She kicked and scratched and spat, but the two men easily subdued her and took their turns slapping her.

"I can hear you men hitting her," a voice called from the direction of the men on horseback. "I hope there won't be any visible marks since she's supposed to be getting married this eve."

One of her captors looked at the other and said, "Enough. I don't wish to be strung up by my bollocks."

"How is this for your bollocks?" Elizabeth asked as she directed a very damaging kick at the spot between his legs. The brute bent over with a yowl faster than she'd expected, though she'd never done such a thing before. It didn't stop the other from hoisting her over his shoulder and carrying her back to the horses to a chorus of cheers and whistles from the group. She was thrown atop a horse in front of the man who'd struck her twice. Someone else tied her hands with rope.

The one she'd kicked was slowly making his way back, his hand protecting his bollocks. The others chided him more than they did Elizabeth.

They headed back to her prison-to-be, and since there was naught else she could do, she was careful to memorize the area, taking note of any landmarks she saw along the way. At least now she'd have an idea who had stolen her. They weren't English, of that she was certain. They wore plaids, but they weren't MacTear colors, though he'd donned his dress colors to Grant Castle, something guards didn't wear.

Two men had Norse accents, but that wasn't unusual. Ever since the Battle of Largs there had been more Norse sprinkled through the Highlands. Her sister-in-law Sela was half Norse.

Perhaps Orvar was involved. It was said that he'd taken over a castle in the Northern Highlands. If so, he would have kept many of the Scots as workers and guards.

She would pay attention when they arrived back at the castle. It was a long ride, a testament to how far she'd traveled on foot. Her feet were now blistered and sore, her wrists raw from the rope, and her hair a mess of waves falling from the tie at her crown.

The bleak towers of a castle stood out against the gray sky, the air misting a wee bit. They approached a small village, and the people who had been out starting their days' work gathered around the path so they could assess the group arriving. It wasn't long before the whispers grew loud enough for her to overhear.

"She's not the bride, is she?"

"How could she be? She looks like a dirty peasant. And just look at her hair."

"They found this one in the woods eating dirt for her meal."

"They say his bride-to-be is a beauty. Surely this cannot be her."

"She's probably a thief."

The guards guffawed at their talk. The one in front of her glanced over his shoulder and said, "I think he'll change his mind about you now, lass. One look at you would send me running."

Elizabeth had never been so humiliated, but she held her head high and stared straight ahead. She vowed not to give in to the tears that threatened to drench her cheeks. Perhaps she'd be fortunate and he'd no longer want her.

She could only hope.

The guards took her through the gates of the curtain wall, through the courtyard, and up to the steps to the keep. She'd hoped to be greeted by her captor, to at last find out who'd stolen her, but there was no sign of him. A large woman awaited them. "Take her to the tower room and lock her inside," she said dismissively. "Everything she needs until the wedding this eve is already there. I'll let him know you've found her." Then her gaze traveled from Elizabeth's head to her toes and she snickered. "Why he wants this one, I'll never know. There are plenty of lovely lasses here he could choose."

"She's a Grant. 'Tis why." The one who held her dragged her through the hall, then up a tightly winding circular staircase, moving so quickly she tripped twice. At this point, she was so exhausted the only thing she would be doing once she got inside the chamber was sleeping.

They stopped in front of a large chamber door at the very top—much too high for her to attempt another escape from the window. The man who'd dragged her removed the rope from her wrists, opened the door with a key, and shoved her inside. He locked it behind her, the sound of the key in the lock reminding her they'd be much more careful this time.

Elizabeth had never felt so lost or forlorn. She rubbed her raw wrists, noticing the dirt covering her everywhere. Removing her mantle, she tossed it on a peg and checked her surroundings, surprised to see the room was a pleasant sort of prison. There was a crackling fire in the hearth, and a tub with steaming water sat in front of it.

While she would have liked to go to her wedding covered in dirt, simply to spite the bastard who'd stolen her, she didn't plan on attending. Her father, her brothers, Gil, and Loki would be storming the place soon. She had faith in her clan. In her love. Removing her boots as gingerly as possible, she stripped off the woolen hose, only to see how much she'd damaged her feet overnight. She counted at least four blisters hidden beneath the dirt that had infiltrated her boots.

While she resented every bit of this situation, a bath would make her feel better, so she decided to take one. And she would devour the tray of fruit and cheese while she soaked in the tub. Hadn't her father always told them that if they were captured, they were to keep their strength up? That doing so was the only way to get out safely?

There were only three small windows. She peeked through one and sighed when she noticed it faced the courtyard. It was so high that she'd probably vomit if she ever had to climb down from such a height. But even her thin frame wouldn't fit through the opening.

She was stuck until her clan found her.

Bath, food, sleep.

There was nothing else she could do.

Gil thought he'd be heaving soon over the side of his horse, though since Phillipa rode behind him, he prayed he wouldn't. What was a man to do when the woman he loved had been kidnapped and he had no idea where she'd been taken, or who'd done the taking?

Three hours after they arrived at Castle Curanta, they set out in the dark in search of any sign of Elizabeth. Loki's plan was to catch up with one of the Grant patrols so they could combine their efforts. The more area they could cover, the better off they would be. Kenzie had improved, but not to the point of being ready for combat, so he'd stayed back to protect the castle with a group of guards.

Gil hadn't wanted to take Phillipa along, but she and Daw had convinced him they could be invaluable. Both knew all the questionable characters in Edinburgh, and they excelled at collecting secret information and could sneak into places the warriors could not. Moreover, it was possible the bastard who'd forced them to steal could be the one who'd kidnapped Elizabeth, and they might recognize his companions.

Of course, that had made it difficult to find solid reasoning for Loki's son, Lucas, who was close to them in age, not to go along with them, but Loki convinced him he was needed at home to protect Castle Curanta. He had been given duty on the curtain wall, something new for him.

Loki had insisted that Gil could not ride alone, what with his wound and his lack of sleep, so Phil was chosen to ride with him. She had been instructed to holler for the closest guard if Gil started to sway.

Two hours after they left Castle Curanta, they caught up with a Grant patrol, the leader conferring with another group. Daw rode with Thorn, who wasn't far from Gil.

"Who is it?" Gil called out to Loki, doing his best to keep his stamina up to stay focused on saving Lizzie.

"I think 'tis Alex Grant speaking to Laird MacTear."

"Why would MacTear be out at this hour?"

"I'm sure he's volunteered to help locate Elizabeth," Loki said. "Word travels fast in the Highlands. He still wishes to take her as his wife, so stopping the culprit would be foremost on his mind. I want to hear who Alex thinks is the guilty party, especially after conferring with MacTear."

"'Tis the baron," Gil said. "I'm sure of it. 'Twill be a long journey to England, but it must be made. I wonder if Jake or Jamie have headed to England ahead of this group."

They approached the gathering just as MacTear motioned for his men to leave. As they passed, Loki yelled out to MacTear. "Godspeed for our Elizabeth, MacTear."

The laird turned back and yelled, "I always have the best of luck. You'll see. I'll find her first." He led his group into a gallop and they headed down the pathway leading south.

Gil didn't want MacTear to find her first. While he should welcome all the help, he would prefer it if the laird went back to his land.

Because if he found her before Gil did, he would have Alex's gratitude, and possibly his blessing.

Alex made his way over closer to their group. "Loki, pleased to see you've brought a fine group of warriors to assist us."

"Of course, Alex. We'll do whatever you wish. Who do you think has kidnapped her? Have you suspicions of one person in particular?"

Alex cast a sideways glance at Gil, who struggled to interpret the look. He decided to be forceful and be heard. While he knew some of the fault for this fiasco lay at his feet, he would do anything to fix it. He loved Lizzie with all his heart. "Laird, I'll help in any way possible."

Alex didn't answer, instead sharing the information he'd gleaned from his sons and MacTear. "MacTear is going after the Norseman, Jake is ahead of us, headed toward England, while Connor has a group searching the periphery of the main routes south, hoping to find some reivers or anyone with information. He'll stop at some of the major clans along the way. Maggie and Will are traveling with him."

"And you?" Loki asked.

"I'm going after the baron, the bastard who I'm sure has her. I'll cut his throat for daring to touch her. Jake will search a few more places, but I head straight for Baron Haite, where Jake will join us."

The two groups shared information, then moved their horses into formation, ready to leave. It was then Phil tugged on the back of Gil's tunic.

He turned around and whispered, "What is it, lass? We have to move along quickly."

"Nay, going to England is wrong. You're going the wrong way. I've been trying to tell you, but you've ignored me."

"Your pardon. My mind is preoccupied." He glanced over his shoulder, pausing his horse for a moment. "Why do you say England is the wrong way?"

"'Tis him. The bastard who made us steal. He's the one who never wanted us to see his face, but I snuck a look at him once in Edinburgh. 'Tis him. And the man next to him was the one whom I overheard. The one who said they'd be stealing a bride later. They're the guilty ones."

"The man who was just here?" Gil couldn't believe his ears, but the lass had promised she was one of the best spies in Edinburgh. He knew Loki had been just as canny while living on the streets of Ayr, and the same was true of Kenzie. Gil himself had helped Kyla and Finlay escape confinement in Buchan Castle. Young ones had a way of getting information others couldn't. "Are you sure, lass? Lizzie's life is at stake. Give me your reasons."

She looked over at Daw, riding with Thorn. "I think so," he

answered, "though 'tis dark and hard to see."

Phil jutted her chin out and said, "I never forget a bastard's face."

Gil had to do something.

"Alex Grant, hold!" His bellow stopped nearly everyone, but Loki just nodded and motioned for him to move closer to Alex. "A word. Could we have a word, please?"

Alex motioned for his men to move ahead, and Loki shifted their warriors off to the side, allowing the two the chance to speak privately between them.

"Gil, I know you have feelings for my daughter, but you cannot allow it to cloud your thinking."

"I understand that, Laird, and you're correct. I love your daughter, and if we find her, I'll be asking your permission to take her as my wife, but this is not the time."

"Then what do you want?"

"This lass has something to say, and I think you need to hear her out."

"Who is she?"

"This is Phil. We found her in Edinburgh. There are men who force the orphans to steal for them, and the coin all goes to one man. She also said that a man who works for him bragged about plans to steal a bride."

Alex moved his horse closer so he could see Phillipa. "Tell me what you know, lass. This is important."

"'Tis him. The one who just left. I never knew his name because 'twas kept secret. But he's the one who came to collect the coin from the ones who made us steal, and his man next to him is the one who said he'd be stealing a bride." Her voice grew more agitated as she spoke. "You must believe me."

"Say I *do* believe you. What makes you think that they'd be stealing my daughter? The man you're accusing is an ally, not an enemy."

"Because he said they were going to steal the most beautiful golden-haired lass in the Highlands. And they said she was tall, and her brothers and father were all tall, too." Her finger came up to her mouth, and she chewed on her fingernail.

"Gil, this is a powerful accusation to make. Are you certain?"

"Aye," Phil blurted out. "I'll tell you how we know!"

"Go on, and it must be true, because if we attack him, there'll be many deaths."

"'Twas what he said. He said the same thing when he picked up money from his men. I wanted to see who he was, so I followed his men and watched from the shadows. He laughed and said, 'I always have the best of luck.' He has a scar above his left brow. I couldn't tell here, but I saw it clearly in Edinburgh. I hate him. He's a cruel man."

Gil looked to Alex for confirmation of the scar.

Loki said, "I've not been that close to him. Alex? 'Struth he has a scar?"

Alex nodded slowly. "He does. I don't have to see it because I know it well. I gave it to him a long time ago. But 'tis above his right eye." He glanced at Phil, waiting for her reaction.

She and Daw both shouted at the same time. "Nay!"

"Phil's correct," Daw added, which had to be the first time the two had agreed on anything. "'Tis his left brow. I saw him once, too. Crooked scar."

"I believe them, laird," Gil said. "If you'll not go that way, I will. They have no reason to lie to you."

Alex smiled, and Loki chuckled. It was as if they'd gone mad, and Gil glanced from one to the other, waiting for them to share the joke.

"Why are you smiling? We must go after her," Phil shouted.

Alex said, "You passed my test, lassie. You and your friend. I believe you. 'Tis indeed his left brow."

"Then what's our plan?" Gil asked. "The more we wait here, the farther they could be traveling. Who knows what they're doing with Lizzie? Or to Lizzie? She could be in a dungeon, in shackles, we don't..."

Alex held a hand up to stop his tirade. The pained look on his face stopped Gil more than his hand. He had to remind himself that he wasn't the only one who cared about Lizzie. Although it felt as if she had been a special part of his life forever, she hadn't. For Alex? She'd been special to him for over two decades.

"The plan is I'm after MacTear for stealing my daughter. If I find out he has her, there is only one possible result."

Gil waited, not wanting to interrupt the man.

Alex said to Phil, "Lass, my thanks to you and your friend. You'll get your reward later."

"Alex, we'll do as you instruct," Gil prompted. "You know MacTear better than any of us. I bow to your expertise, Laird."

"The only instruction you need is that MacTear is mine. Gil, we have to save Elizabeth. 'Tis due time for a wedding."

CHAPTER EIGHTEEN

FOLLOWING MACTEAR'S TRACKS was easy since it was a dewy morn. It was quite telling that while he'd headed south for a while, he'd turned and taken a well-hidden path to his own land.

Gil prayed they arrived in time, that they could stop a wedding from happening, if that was what MacTear had planned. The truth was they had no idea what he would do. It would be nearly high sun by the time they arrived at his castle. If they were successful, they'd have her home by nightfall.

As they rode, Gil kept his hand on the bandage over his wound. Visions of Morgan's face still haunted him. Could it truly have been him? He chided himself for being ridiculous. After all these years, what were the chances? Though he tried his best to ignore the gash, it continued to pain him something fierce.

After a time, Alex slowed his horse and came abreast of Loki, Gil, and Thorn. "I'm more convinced than ever of the bastard's guilt. He planned his ruse cleverly, and it would have worked if not for Phil." He nodded to her. "Unfortunately for him, men that spend much of their time crawling on their bellies as serpents eventually get caught. But this is not going to be an easy battle. This man is a snake, and we will have to outsmart his trickery. I believe, without a doubt, that Elizabeth is being kept inside his castle and I would wager the priest is there to perform the wedding as soon as MacTear returns. Stealing a bride is not a crime once the vows have been said."

Gil's gut churned at the thought. "Then we cannot wait. How would you suggest we do this? Perhaps I should infiltrate the castle and search it while you confront MacTear and his men. I'm afraid I'll not be much of a swordsman in my condition."

Alex nodded, considering his proposal, his hard gaze on Gil. "I'll go along with that suggestion, but you are to take Phil and Daw with you. They'll be able to get into places you cannot, and if anything happens to you, they'll get back to us."

He faced Phil first. "Do you accept this challenge, lass?"

Her face lit up and she quickly replied, "Aye, Chief!"

Then he did the same with Daw, who gave him another enthusiastic agreement.

His attention shifted to Loki. "I will make a direct challenge to MacTear to fight for my daughter's hand. I'll ask you and Thorn to stay behind me, but only to protect me from anyone who tries to attack me blindly. He will attempt to win by unjust means. I may have to play with him a wee bit to give Gil the chance to search the castle. Once he's dead, many will run inside to hide."

"And if you need me to step in, I'll be at the ready whenever," Loki said. "We could both play with the bastard."

"He *is* a bastard," Phil said, "but is he not a strong swordsman? He said he was the best."

Gil chuckled, and others joined him. "He'd never beat Alex. He's the finest swordsman in the Highlands, and the two next best are Loki and Alex's son Connor."

Alex called to the guard closest to him. "Return to Grant land with five guards and bring two hundred guards back with you. Have Jamie send a messenger to Jake, Connor, and Magnus that we've caught the guilty party."

Hope swelled in Gil's chest. They were close to the end of this, and with all of them working together, they would save Elizabeth. They had to.

Alex called all in for a short blessing, then said, "The Lord will lead us to my daughter. We go in quietly. I know MacTear land well, so when I motion to you, Gil, you're to tie your horse up in a clearing and lead Phil and Daw into the keep through the back wall."

Gil nodded and whispered, "Hold on, Lizzie, we're coming."

Alex stared at him in shock. "She allows you to call her Lizzie?" He arched a brow and shook his head slightly. "She really must love you."

Elizabeth awakened when the sun was nearly high. Dressed in a night rail, she peeked out the window, surprised to see chaos in the courtyard. The din in the bailey had grown over the past hour, making her wonder what this was about. Something was happening, though she knew not what.

Could she dare hope the Grant warriors had arrived so soon?

She had to be ready in case she was rescued, so she quickly dropped the night rail and raced over to her clothing. Her intention had been to don the disheveled pieces, but they were so torn and dirty she couldn't bear to put them on. The only other garment she could find, besides the gown she was to marry in, which she refused to wear, was a lad's outfit in one of the chests.

The outfit didn't fit quite right—the trews were a bit snug and the tunic too loose—but it worked well enough.

The din in the courtyard grew, so she peeked out the window, squinting because of the distance, and gasped at what she saw. There he was, standing in the middle of the chaos, giving orders to men who raced off in several different directions—some ascending the curtain wall, others mounting horses, and still others donning mail.

MacTear! MacTear was the one who'd kidnapped her.

She held her breath as she stared out the window, waiting to see what would happen next, only to let out a sharp squeal of glee when she saw the Grant plaids arrive outside the gates, about two score of them.

She recognized her father in the lead, along with Loki, Thorn, and several of her sire's favorite warriors.

Where was Gil? Her stomach dropped at the thought that he hadn't been well enough to come. She reminded herself that it didn't mean anything bad had happened to him, just that he wasn't strong enough to hold a sword.

When she'd last seen him, he hadn't been strong enough to climb off a pallet, so she forced herself not to consider the worst. He was at Castle Curanta healing, and that was that.

Letting out the breath she'd been holding, she pulled back the fur and focused on the activity down below. How she wished she could hear their conversation, but there was too much noise from the crowd.

Tears filled her eyes as she watched her sire dismount his horse and slowly stride over to stand in front of MacTear, Loki and Thorn following him at a slight distance. The crowd finally quieted as everyone strained to hear what was being said. Elizabeth bit back tears so she wouldn't miss a word.

"Where is my daughter? Release her now, MacTear."

"Are you addled, Grant? She's not here. We already discussed this. Go search the Norseman's land." MacTear stood on the platform in the middle of the courtyard, but her father was so tall he could nearly look him in the eye anyway. MacTear began to ramble. "Or go to the baron. He already tried to steal her once. He must be the guilty party. I'm your neighbor. I wouldn't act against you."

Dead silence from the crowd.

Her father merely looked at him. It must have been one of his severe looks because the bastard couldn't stop his rambling. "Had I any knowledge of her location, I would have told you when we met a few hours ago. I searched but found nothing, so we returned to the castle for rest and the midday meal."

If it were possible for a man to squirm while standing, MacTear was attempting it. He looked as uncomfortable as anyone she'd ever seen, but he held his position.

Her father's voice came out in a dead serious tone his children had all learned to dread. This time Elizabeth silently applauded. "I know she's here, you bastard," he bellowed, stepping closer to MacTear. "Release her now or the battle will commence. I just sent for five hundred more warriors to add to the two hundred I brought with me." Elizabeth knew one of his usual tactics was to overstate his numbers, but she suspected he probably *had* sent for more warriors.

MacTear's hands came up, his palms facing her father. "Alex, your worry has turned you daft. I swear to you she's not here." The courtyard was the quietest it had been yet, MacTear's entire clan waiting for her father's response.

Elizabeth leaned out the window as far as she could and bellowed, "Papa! Papa! I'm here! Please! He has me locked in the tower."

Her father looked up at her, but the crowd remained quiet. "There's confirmation of your lie. I'll ask you one more time, MacTear. Release my daughter, or face my wrath."

"Go home, Grant. The priest has already married us. She's mine now."

"Nay, he's lying, Papa. Never! Never will I marry him." Her voice carried across the courtyard.

The next sound to meet her ears was of all the Grant warriors unsheathing their swords at once. "One to one, MacTear. I challenge you for my daughter. Here and now. You have one minute to choose your weapon."

The crowd began to stir, and MacTear pulled his sword out as he jumped off the platform. But rather than meet the challenge like a man, he attempted to move away. Her father pursued him, of course, and MacTear pretended he wouldn't fight back. He practically dropped to his knees—then brought his sword up, aimed straight at Alex's midsection.

Elizabeth screamed.

It was happening again, and there was nothing she could do to stop it.

CHAPTER NINETEEN

GIL STOOD OUTSIDE the back of the curtain wall, turning to Phil and Daw. "We have to make a plan. My guess is she's in one of the towers, but she could be in the dungeons. We'll have to split up. Can you go alone," he asked Phil, "or do you and Daw wish to travel together?"

Phil said, "Alone," at the same exact time Daw said, "Together."

Gil arched his brow at the two but made his decision. He could hear the dull roar of the crowd building, which suggested everyone was leaving the castle to witness the arrival of the Grant warriors and the confrontation.

It was their best chance to get in.

"You'll go together and search the dungeon. Be careful. If one of you gets caught, the other must come and find me. And if she's not down there, make your way to the towers. It won't take Alex long to challenge MacTear."

The two nodded and they snuck inside the wall, surprised to find the door unlocked and the area empty. They crept past the kitchens, again seeing no one, although the roar of the crowd indicated everyone was in front of the castle.

Gil found the stairway to the dungeons and sent the two down, pointing out the entrance to the two different towers before sending them on their way. He made his way to the first tower and found it deserted, the door at the top open. Lizzie couldn't be inside, unless she was tied to the bed, but he'd wager she'd still find a way out. So he turned and ran for the other tower.

Alex's voice rang out, followed by MacTear's weak denials. He also made the mistake of calling Alex addled. If he were a wagering man, Gil would have bet that insult would cost him another arm.

Sneaking over to the other tower and encountering no one, he hesitated at the base of the circular staircase. The upper door was closed, and he could make out what looked to be a key in the lock. He rushed up just as he heard Lizzie yelling out to her father. The quiet outside turned into a melee, and he raced up the staircase, three steps at a time, turning the key and opening the door.

Lizzie screamed as she leaned over the windowsill. "Papa, nay!"

"Lizzie," he called out, rushing to her side.

She spun around and squealed, "Gil!" Then she threw herself into his arms and burst into tears. He kissed her cheek and her forehead and every part of her he could.

"You are hale? He did not harm you?" Gil couldn't stop touching her to assure himself she was safe. His wound forgotten, he hugged her and held her, murmuring, "I love you, Lizzie. I meant what I said in Edinburgh. Marry me, and I'll live wherever you wish. I need you."

She nodded, her sobs hitching, but she kissed his lips, tasting him briefly before she pulled back. "I have a few small wounds, but I'll be fine. Papa is fighting MacTear, and he was almost struck down."

She grabbed his hand and pulled him over to the window just as Daw and Phil came in through the door. "You found her," Phil said, with a firm nod.

"Papa is fighting him. He could die," she said to the three of them, as if they could stop it from happening.

Gil peered out the window while Daw and Phil climbed onto a chest to look out another window.

Lizzie latched on to him and sobbed. "Papa's going to die. Look at how close the sword comes to him." She leaned out the window and screamed, although it likely could not be heard over the new tumult in the courtyard.

"Lizzie, come away from there," he said. "He's not dying. You'll distract him, and then he'll make a mistake."

"Nay," Daw yelled excitedly, "she could never distract the great Alexander Grant. Look at him fight! I've never seen anyone fight like that. He'll surely win. He's just taunting MacTear now. Just look at how much taller he is. And the size of his arms!"

"He's my father. He cannot die because of me. I cannot lose him. Gil, you must do something!" She grasped his shoulders and stared up at him, giving him a desperate look that went straight to his heart, but he had faith in Alexander Grant.

He tugged her away from the window and wrapped his arms around her, giving him the view from the window. "Have you never seen him in a swordfight before?"

"Nay, Mama has always kept me away. I've seen him in the lists, but this is different. He could die," she cried, leaning her head on his shoulder and closing her eyes.

He whispered into her ear. "Your sire is the most powerful swordsman in all the land. Do not fear for him, but I must watch for any trickery. Your father warned Loki about it."

"And look at Loki fighting too," Daw said. "He's so fast! And now more Grant warriors are coming. They're taking over. We'll win! We'll will!"

"Then please watch for me, because I cannot," Lizzie said, burying her face in the crick of his neck while her hand squeezed the back of his neck.

Alex was backed up to the curtain wall, which was why he noticed them so quickly—a group of three men pushing something down the walkway on the wall, moving in *his* direction. Gil couldn't believe his eyes, but he'd not let Lizzie know what he saw.

A pot of boiling oil meant for Alex Grant.

He'd heard of others pouring boiling oil on their enemies, but the Grants never committed such a despicable practice.

"Daw, Phil, take Lizzie downstairs to the great hall. The fight will be over in a few minutes, and she can greet her father then. Lizzie, go with them and don't look outside. Promise me you'll wait until the fight is over." He held her in front of him, his hands gripping her shoulders. "Promise me, please."

"All right, I promise, but are you not going with us?" she asked, wiping her tears.

"Nay, I have one more thing I must do. Now, you must wait two minutes before you go. Understood?"

"Aye, we'll do it, Master Gil," Daw said.

Gil didn't tell any of them what he'd seen, but he had to get to the entrance to the parapets and follow the curtain wall around to stop them. He raced down the stairs to the other tower, where he'd noticed a door to the parapets. Once outside, he set his hand on his sword, ready to unsheathe it as he moved closer, but panic unfurled within him. He wasn't moving quickly enough.

"Alex Grant, get away from the wall!" he bellowed as he continued to run. "Move!"

But even if the Grant had heard him, he couldn't change his position—there were too many swordsmen in the courtyard. Then Gil had a sudden inspiration. He'd nearly reached the corner of the parapets so he had to back up to give himself the shot he needed.

He pulled out his slinger and selected a stone from his pocket to do the most serious damage, aimed, and fired across the wall, exhilarated when it struck one of the guards between his eyes, the force making him take his hands off the pot as he stumbled backward, falling over the back of the wall. Taking another stone out, he prepared to fire at the guard on the other side, only someone else did it first. The man stumbled backward, then fell over the edge. The third began to run away, but Gil hit him square on his temple and he crumpled to the walkway.

Gil could have shouted for joy, but where had the other stone come from? Looking around, he heard a loud whistle from beneath him. When he glanced down, he saw Loki standing on the platform with a wide grin on his face. He gave a quick bow before he took his sword out again.

The battle was nearly over. MacTear dropped his sword and held his arms up in surrender, so Alex instructed his men to tie him up and place him atop a horse.

He'd be sending him to a magistrate to be arrested and sent to England in shame. Gil made his way to the other exit since it was closer, racing down the steps and landing outside the curtain wall. He wove his way through the small crowd of villagers, heading back into the courtyard now flooded with Grant warriors. He was nearly halfway across it when he heard someone off to the side holler at him.

"Had to be quite a wound to make you limp like that."

Gil froze. The voice was familiar.
He turned around and there he was.
Morgan.

CHAPTER TWENTY

ONLY IT WASN'T Morgan. Up close, he realized the man he'd seen at the market in Edinburgh, the one who'd stabbed him, was just an uncanny look alike.

He stood in the corner of the courtyard, away from the chaos, another man directly behind him.

Gil moved over slowly, doing his best to hide his limp. He didn't need to hear their chuckles to know he'd failed.

"You done a good job, Herman," the second man said.

Gil moved to stand directly in front of the fool. He was medium height, bald, with a full beard. He looked as though he'd had a muscular build earlier in life, but no longer. Gil put him at around thirty winters, someone who lived a lazy life, winding down in his ability to be a strong warrior. "I have you to thank for this injury, Herman? Who *are* you? And who's your friend hiding behind you?"

Herman came up to Gil, his attitude surprisingly confident for a man who was a head shorter than him. "Jasper is a fine help to me," he said, "but leave him out of any discussion we have. He doesn't know the answers."

From the way Jasper hung back behind his friend, it was obvious he accepted the other man was in charge.

They reminded him so much of Horas and Morgan, it was hard to see them as they were and not as the two men from his past. "I'll repeat my question. Why me?"

"You took the bairns," Jasper said, surprising him by answering. "Couldn't let word get around about what the laird was doing. Said we were to kill anyone that took them. We did the best we could."

Shock roiled through Gil. These were the men who'd used and manipulated Herry and Daw for MacTear. The bastards. Jasper pulled a dagger from his boot, and Gil couldn't help but wonder exactly what he planned to do with that weapon.

Herman spat off to the side, his hand reaching into his boot as if Gil wouldn't notice. "We were pleased enough to get to attack a group of Grant warriors. We don't want you Highland savages in Edinburgh. Take a hint and stay away."

His anger flared even higher. "If you hate us so, why work for a Highlander? Why come into the Highlands?"

He knew it wasn't them he was asking for answers. Not really. These men had used orphans to do their bidding. In a strange way, it felt like this was his chance to confront the men who'd made his life miserable.

It was likely the only chance he'd ever get.

"Because MacTear was looking for men to fight the Grants, and we were wanting to settle a grudge. If not for the Grants and Ramsays, we'd still be making coin from the Channel of Dubh."

He referred to the network of kidnappers who'd stolen lasses and lads and sent them across the seas to be traded as property. Gil felt himself bristle further.

He smirked, holding his arms up and spreading them wide. "Did you expect you could truly beat us in the Highlands? Alex Grant just won. Your leader is restrained, and I doubt he'll be any help to you now.

He thought again about Daw and Herry, about what they'd likely been through with these men. "Did you slap the lads you forced to steal for MacTear?"

"Aye, and they deserve it. Wise arses, the lot of them. Daw was stupid to get himself caught by you. I'd leather him good if I could."

Gil saw red. For a moment, he thought he'd snap the bastard's neck. "Herry, too? Did you hit him?"

Jasper laughed and said, "He always cried like a wee bairn when Herman struck him."

"Herry *is* a bairn, you daft arse," Gil growled, grabbing Herman by the tunic and punching him square in the face, hearing a resounding snap when he connected with his nose. "This is for punching bairns. How does it feel?" He punched him in his belly and then his side before shoving him backward and kicking him straight into a pile of horse dung.

Then he went after Jasper, who turned wide-eyed and yellow-bellied. "I didn't stab you! And Herman hit the lads. Not me!"

"You lie," Herman yelled. "You liked hitting them more than I did. I did it for discipline. You did it because you enjoyed it."

"That makes it your turn to see how it feels." He threw three punches at Jasper and then stepped back, now heaving.

Loki came up next to him. "Found someone you know, aye? Would you like some assistance? Since you have that wound in your leg, Thorn and I would be pleased to finish it for you."

Jasper screamed and ran, blood pouring from his nose. Herman had only managed to roll out of the dung. He still hadn't stood up.

Loki went over and pulled the man to his feet. "I don't know who the hell you are, but if I ever see your face in the Highlands again. I'll bring you to the Grant lists for target practice. Understood?"

Then he turned and surveyed all the Grant warriors gathered in the courtyard. "Or would you like to try now? There's enough of us to make it a good game of it, aye?"

Herman whimpered like a wee bairn, shaking his head, and Loki tossed him across the field.

He clasped Gil's shoulder and took a look at his fist, the knuckles a little scraped from the battering he'd given them. "Hurt bad?"

Gil smiled. "Hell, nay. Felt great."

Lizzie paced inside, listening to the battle sounds, which had steadily dissipated. Daw and Phil were peeking out the door, keeping her abreast of everything. "My father? Is he still standing?"

Daw turned around, grinning. "Shite, no one could stop him. Why are you worried? The battle is mostly over."

"Do you see Gil anywhere?"

"Aye," Phil said. "He was just up on the battlements. He stopped three of MacTear's men from pouring boiling oil on your sire."

"Boiling oil? On my sire?" That was it. She couldn't wait any longer. She pushed past the two, shoving the door open, and charged through the courtyard, grateful she had trews on instead of a gown.

The men were so tall, she couldn't see over many of them, but the Grant warriors recognized her and opened a path up for her straight to her father. "Papa! Papa!"

She ran toward him, tears blurring her vision as she finally reached him. He stood by the gates, giving orders to his men. "Papa!"

Her father opened his arms to her, and she launched herself at him, throwing her arms around his neck and blubbering unlike she'd ever done before. "I was so frightened watching you fight."

Once she was a wee bit calmer, he set her feet back on the ground and checked her over. "Did he harm you, lass? Any of them?"

"Nay, Papa. I'm fine."

He set his finger under her chin, lifting her face so he could take a closer look. "Where did you get the cuts on your face then?"

"Cuts? Oh, must be from when I escaped last eve. I ran through the forest and couldn't see in the dark, so I got caught by the brambles. Are there that many?"

Her father just arched his brow at her, and she scowled, wondering why Gil hadn't said anything.

"Papa, have you seen Gil? Is he hale?"

"Aye, he's over there giving a couple of fools a battering with his fists. Even with a slice in his leg that nearly cut it in two, he's still able to handle two men by himself. I guess he'll be able to protect my daughter, should he choose to ask for your hand, Lizzie." He put particular emphasis on the nickname, which she'd asked everyone in the family to stop using when she was ten summers.

"He's the only one I allow to call me that, Papa," she said, lifting her brow.

"Don't I know it. I remember when you said we all had to stop calling you that. It switched to Eliza and then Liz and then none." He crossed his arms and looked down at her with such emotion it nearly choked her up.

"I love you, Papa. I don't like watching you fight."

"Your mother has coddled you in that respect, but I'm quite proud of you for escaping. How did you get out of the tower? 'Tis a long drop, lass."

"I was on the second floor. I waited until dark and then tied the ropes from the canopy together, climbed out the window, and went out the back wall. I wasn't going to marry him, Papa. Gil is to be my husband."

He gave her another odd look, then leaned down and kissed the top of her head. "I guess I'll have to finally let you go, daughter, but I'll always love you. You knew we'd come, didn't you?"

"Aye, but I thought I was in England."

Her father drawled, "So did I."

Gil appeared behind her father with Loki and Thorn next to him. She shifted, ready to run to him, but he shook his head. The longing in his eyes told her that he had only held back out of respect for her father, so she listened.

Her father turned around. "Who do I have to thank for stopping the pot of boiling oil from pouring on my head?"

Loki and Thorn both pointed at Gil.

"Stone from his slinger hit one of them right between the eyes," Thorn said.

Gil added, "Loki must have heard me because he took out the second one."

"My thanks to both of you." Then he narrowed his attention on Gil. "You met someone from your past over there in the corner?"

Gil nodded. "The man who stabbed me in Edinburgh. Says they don't like Grant warriors down south. They worked for MacTear. They're the ones who got the bairns to steal for him in Edinburgh."

"But why stab you?" Elizabeth asked.

"Said that MacTear told them not to let any of the bairns get carried off. He was afraid he'd be tied back to it. Turns out they don't much like the Grants either. They were tied up with the Channel of Dubh."

Her father lifted Gil's battered hand and looked at it. "They like to batter bairns, aye? I wondered why you weren't using your sword or dagger on them, but this felt much better, didn't it? Fair is fair."

Gil grinned and nodded. "Sure did, my laird."

Phillipa and Daw came up behind them, and Phil asked, "'Tis over?"

"Aye," Alex answered. "The battle is done, lass, and the MacTear will have his title stripped. By the way, Elizabeth—" He looked down at her. "If not for Gil, Phil, and Daw, I'd still be headed into England after the baron. I couldn't believe MacTear had turned against me."

"Mama won't be happy," she said.

He gave her a strange look, then shook his head slightly. "Oh, I think she will be." He shifted his attention back to the orphans then, and said, "I owe you both a debt of gratitude, and I hope you and Daw will join Clan Grant. Your choice if you'd rather stay with us or with Loki at Castle Curanta."

The two bounced up and down in excitement.

"You can decide later, after the celebration this eve at Grant Castle for my daughter's return. Now, daughter, are you going to thank this man for the role he played in saving both of our lives?"

Elizabeth grinned as she raced to Gil, wrapping her arms around his neck and kissing him. It was a quick kiss, but then Elizabeth glanced over her shoulder at her sire, who was now looking at the surrounding area, so she kissed him again, slipping her tongue into his mouth quickly.

He stopped the kiss and glared at her, angling his eyes toward her father.

Her laughter was the most beautiful sound he'd ever heard.

CHAPTER TWENTY-ONE

THE GRANT WAR whoop echoed out over the land as Jake and Connor arrived with more Grant guards.

The worst was finally over.

They arranged to have Magnus escort MacTear to the magistrate, along with some of his men. The rest would be settled under Grant guards until word came back from Edinburgh. Gil settled Lizzie on his horse, then mounted behind her. Before the horse could take a single step, Alex Grant came bounding up next to them on his warhorse.

He held his hand out to his daughter. "Sorry, Gil, but this honor still belongs to me." Then he gave his daughter a look she'd never seen, one of a vulnerable man. "Elizabeth, I feared I'd lost you, one way or the other. Do an old man a favor."

"Oh, Papa, you'll make me cry."

Gil didn't hesitate. He lifted Elizabeth, his strong, capable hands wrapped around her waist, and settled her in front of her father.

They rode back, Jamie, Jake, and Connor in the lead, with Alex, Loki, Thorn, and Gil behind them. About ten score of warriors took up the rear of the group. It was a ride of joy and celebration, though it would take them a couple of hours to reach the castle.

When they were far enough from the others not to be overheard, her father said, "Now I'd like to hear just exactly what this lad means to you. I'm going to lose you to him, am I not?"

Elizabeth's eyes misted immediately. "Nay, Papa. You'll never lose me. Gil and I have been together for about six or seven moons. We spent time together at Castle Curanta, and it just happened. Seeing how hard he works, his patience with the bairns, his sense of humor…I just fell for him." She turned around to look up at her sire. "Papa, he reminds me of you, honorable and strong, gentle and loving, yet a fine warrior. You know Loki considers him one of his best warriors. 'Tis how he ended up in Edinburgh."

"Lass, I understand young love as I remember it verra well, but why have you not shared this with your mother and me? Why hasn't he done the right thing and asked me for your hand?"

"Papa, 'tis all my fault. I wouldn't let him. He wanted to, but we both are happy where we are. He feels devoted to Loki and some of the bairns there. And I…I…"

She turned around and leaned back against her sire, unable to say the words. Grateful the mood was boisterous enough so no one could overhear their conversation, she fought back tears, swallowing hard.

"Lass, tell me how it was your fault, please?"

She turned sideways to try to explain it to him. "Papa, I was afraid to leave you. The thought of leaving Grant Castle…it broke my heart." Her tears started and she couldn't stop them. "I had to stay behind when you were hurt. Mama always hides everything from me, and I never know the truth of what is happening to you or Jake or Jamie or Connor. The only way I find out is if I'm there. I didn't think I could leave you and Mama, but…"

"But?"

She peeked back over her shoulder at him. "But after all this, I'm not sure anymore. I need to be with Gil, wherever we live. I love him, and I was so scared for him when he was hurt. When I arrived in Edinburgh, I thought he would die. And then I was attacked, and I woke up in a room in this castle. I knew not if he lived or died. Even when I looked out of the tower, I wasn't sure if he was alive because he wasn't with you. I was so frightened. But I need him, I need to be with him all the time. I'm sorry, Papa, but now I know what I want, and it's Gil."

"You know what's happened?"

"Nay, Papa. I'm more confused than ever. Everything has turned upside-down on me. My simple, orderly life has become a world of chaos, and I don't know where to go from here."

Pride shone in his eyes. "What's happened is my wee lassie has grown up to be a woman. You know what's in your heart, you just have to reach for it."

"I do love him so."

"Your mama and I will be fine. You may choose to live wherever you would like. 'Tis your choice. Together."

"But he has to ask you for my hand first. I know he will."

"He already did, but it wasn't the best situation, so he'll ask again, I'm sure. Until then, we're nearly on Grant land, so you know what that means, do you not?"

"Aye, I'm home finally." She sat up straight and swiped at the tears running down her cheeks.

"Cover your ears, lass. We just crossed the border, and 'tis time to let Maddie know you're safe."

Her father let out a loud war whoop and her brothers all followed suit, setting their horses into a gallop across the meadow and up the hill to Grant Castle, their banners hoisted in the air. The noise from all the warriors causing such a din that she did indeed cover her ears, laughing as her father sent Midnight into a full gallop. "Hang on, lassie. We won."

She giggled as they trounced across the meadow, watching Gil out of the corner of her eye. She knew he was still in a great deal of pain, but he was smiling at her like she'd just become his betrothed. How she wished it were true.

When they arrived outside the gates, she could see her mother standing at the opening waiting for them, Maeve and Kyla next to her. A line of stable lads awaited the horses.

Tears streamed down her mother's face, but she was smiling. Kyla whooped as loudly as one of the men, and Maeve hooked her arm through Mama's, both of them crying now.

Once they were close enough, her father lowered her down and she raced to her mother, throwing her arms around her.

"Thank the Lord you are home safe, Elizabeth. You were not harmed?"

"Nay, Mama, I'm fine. I've never been happier." She gave her mother another squeeze, then embraced her two sisters.

Kyla frowned, giving her an odd look. "What happened to your face?"

Maeve forced a smile. "I think she looks fine."

"Thanks to you, Maeve. It was dark, and I ran into a few tree branches, but it does not matter. Gil is fine and I'm in love with him and I'm safe and all will be well."

Elizabeth's nephews, her wee protectors, wiggled, pushed, and squirmed their way in front of their grandmother, wooden swords at the ready. Kyla glanced at Alick and said, "Now what have you three planned?"

"Mama, we have to protect Aunt Elizabeth. They could come back for her."

Sela made her way over to Elizabeth and gave her a swift hug. "So happy you're home." Dyna, who'd been standing with her mother, joined the three lads.

"I think you're a little late, lads," she drawled. "You're no longer needed. Gil is Elizabeth's protector now and he has been for several moons."

Elizabeth stared at Dyna, wondering how she could know such a thing, since she'd been too far away to overhear her last comments to her mother. Being with Gil was not a surprise, but the other part was not common knowledge yet. She glanced at Kyla, then her mother and Maeve but they all looked as confused as she did. "Sela? Did you say something to her?"

"Hellfire, nay. She tells me more than I tell her these days."

Dyna looked up at all her elders and smiled, something she didn't do often. "The wedding will be fun."

Her mother wrapped her in a warm embrace and said, "I'm so happy you've found someone, Elizabeth."

"It surely was not MacTear," Dyna said with a snort. "I told you he had bad inside him."

Elizabeth stared at the lass. She had indeed warned her.

Perhaps it was time for them all to start listening to her.

CHAPTER TWENTY-TWO

GIL CELEBRATED OUTSIDE with all the warriors, but as soon as he caught sight of Alex alone, he hurried over to him. "Laird, may I have a word with you in private?"

Alex nodded. "Follow me." He led him through the crowded courtyard, everyone stepping aside to make way for the former laird, and Gil was pleased to receive several pats on the back as he followed him.

They entered the solar, and Alex closed the door after Gil entered, pointing to a chair for him before he took a seat behind one of the desks. The solar had been expanded not long ago to accommodate all three brothers along with their father.

"I was hoping you wouldn't wait long," Alex said with a flat expression.

Gil could feel the sweat in his palms and the twist deep in his gut, but he had to do this. "My lord, I'd like to ask for your daughter's hand in marriage. I love her with all my heart, and I believe I can protect her. I'll always treat her well."

Alex leaned back in his chair and steepled his fingers in front of him. "A few questions first if you don't mind."

"Of course. I'll answer anything for you if I can."

"I'd like to know more about your background. How exactly did you end up at Buchan Castle?"

He told him the whole story, from his parents' and sister's deaths to the promises de La Porte had made and the meat pie that had seemed impossibly big to a hungry orphan. He shrugged. "He promised a good life at the castle to many of us lads. Said he'd make us warriors. I accepted. I was chosen to help Simon because I was small back then, and two other men decided beating on me would be their entertainment. I helped Finlay and Kyla escape, and I will forever be grateful to Finlay for allowing me to come along with them."

Alex studied him for a moment, his scrutiny unnerving. "So that tells me that your constitution was formed by two good parents. You were raised well, and you did the right thing. So why wait so long to ask for my daughter's hand?"

Gil thought long and hard before he answered, a lump in his throat telling him it was time to admit the truth to this man. "I was afraid of your answer. I didn't think I'd be good enough for your daughter. With barons and lairds all pursuing her, how could I measure up?"

Alex moved around to the front of the desk and leaned back against it, crossing his arms in front of him. "Gil, I recall a time when a young lad bravely came into the middle of a sea of mighty warriors to tell me he knew where to find my eldest daughter. You led me to her, and when I found her, she'd told me you were the one who'd saved her life. Were you not the protector of my daughter Kyla when we first met?"

Gil, humbled by this praise, mumbled, "Aye, my lord."

"Then I believe I can trust you to protect this daughter as well. I'd be honored to have you as a son-in-law. Stand up, please."

Gil did as instructed and squared his shoulders to stand in front of the mighty swordsman.

"You have my permission to marry my daughter, if she'll have you. I don't care if you live at Castle Curanta or here, but no farther, please. With our king dead and the English bastards attempting to take control of our verra lives, I'd prefer for my daughters to remain in the Highlands. Will you agree to this?"

"Aye, Laird. And I will treat her with honor and respect at all times."

"I know you will, Gil. Now, when will you propose to ask her so we can announce the betrothal?"

Gil smiled, suddenly feeling lighter than ever. He'd already asked her twice, but this time he'd do it with her sire's permission, and that made all the difference. Still, he'd have to do it differently this time. "How does now sound?"

Alex smiled and clasped his shoulder. "That pleases me verra much. Go find her."

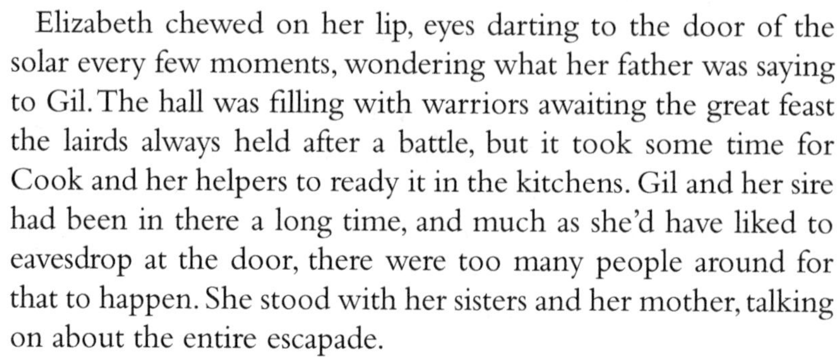

Elizabeth chewed on her lip, eyes darting to the door of the solar every few moments, wondering what her father was saying to Gil. The hall was filling with warriors awaiting the great feast the lairds always held after a battle, but it took some time for Cook and her helpers to ready it in the kitchens. Gil and her sire had been in there a long time, and much as she'd have liked to eavesdrop at the door, there were too many people around for that to happen. She stood with her sisters and her mother, talking on about the entire escapade.

Her mother said, "I still cannot believe MacTear kidnapped you. I was so wrong about him. Did you know it was him, Elizabeth, when he stole you away?"

Elizabeth glanced at the door to the solar again.

"Elizabeth?"

She jerked her gaze back to her mother smoothing her still wild tresses. "Sorry, Mama. Nay, I didn't know. They knocked me over the head, and I lost my senses. When I awakened, I was in a chamber, but no one would tell me whose castle it was."

"And you got to watch Papa fight? Was that not exciting?" Kyla asked. "I love watching him fight."

That caught her attention. "Nay, I hated it. I leaned out of the tower window and screamed. I kept telling him to watch out. Gil finally pulled me away."

Kyla tugged on a few of the waves hanging from the tie at Elizabeth's crown. "'Tis quite a unique hair arrangement you have. Did someone do that for you?"

She could tell her sister did her best not to insult her outright because their mother was there, so she pulled the strands of her hair free. "I had little to use, and I wanted it out of the way when I climbed out the window."

Kyla's entire face lit up. "You tried to escape? What happened? Do tell!"

"There's little to tell except I waited for the middle of the night, then tied ropes together and went out the window. I snuck through the door in the back wall. I had no horse so I had to run in these awful boots and my feet are blistered. Besides, they caught me and dragged me back."

"You poor thing, Elizabeth," her mother said, shaking her head.

Kyla clearly took a different view of it. "Did you get any good punches in? Kick them with your boots?"

Elizabeth had forgotten the one kick that had hit its mark. "I did do one that was quite successful. I kicked him in his…"

Her mother's gaze stopped her from finishing, changing the topic as skillfully as ever. "I do wonder how your father discovered it was MacTear who'd stolen you," her mother said thoughtfully. "I'll have to ask him later."

Finally, after what felt like years of watching, the door to the solar opened and Gil came out, her father behind him.

"They're both smiling," Kyla whispered, "so 'tis good news."

Gil said something to Alex, then strode over to the dais, climbing it and standing up in front of everyone. A wave of his hand silenced the crowd.

"Oh my, Elizabeth," Maeve whispered. "What does this mean?"

"Shush!" was all she could say.

Gil said to the crowd, "I wish to thank everyone who was involved in helping us find Elizabeth and get her away from MacTear. This journey taught me the importance of having the support of one's clan. But more importantly—" he turned to face Elizabeth, "—it taught me that I never want to be away from you again. That I wish to stop hiding our relationship, that I want everyone to see how strong our love is, and I…" His throat caught as he saw her eyes misting. "Wish more than anything to ask her to marry me. Elizabeth Grant, I love you with all my heart. Would you do me the honor of becoming my wife?"

The crowd erupted into a squeal that was quickly hushed as they awaited Elizabeth's answer. She rushed over to the dais, and he helped her up. Laughter burbled from somewhere deep inside of her, a joyful sound. "You are truly asking me a third time? Of course, I will. I'll be your proud wife, live wherever you'd like, have our bairns. I just need to be with you, Gil. All the time. My answer is a resounding aye!"

Applause and screams erupted through the crowd. They hugged and kissed, but then she tugged him down from the dais so they could blend into the now exuberant crowd. She had to ask him a few questions and would prefer not to do it in front of a crowd. "Papa approved? Why were you in there so long?"

He tipped his head and said, "Because the man was finally able to get the truth from me."

"What truth?"

He took her hands and stared at the floor for a moment. "You already know this, but I feared I wouldn't measure up. That your sire wouldn't accept me because I came to Clan Grant as an orphan. But he sees things differently than I did, and I'm grateful he took the time to sit with me. Your sire is one of the most honorable men I've ever met."

Her heart was so full that she wished this moment would last forever. "I love you, Gil, and your worth runs so much deeper than any title could." She ran her fingertips across his lower lip.

"I love you, too, Lizzie. I want you to be in my arms every night and the first thing I see every morning. We are perfect together." He kissed her, this time deeply.

They'd found a secluded corner of the hall, and she'd thought they had all the privacy in the world.

She was wrong.

As soon as their lips touched, the great hall exploded with cheers again.

Since they'd spent so long hiding, it felt just about perfect.

CHAPTER TWENTY-THREE

THE NEXT MORN, Gil and Elizabeth were just finishing their morning meal when the door flew open and a flurry of people entered. The group was from Castle Curanta, and while most of the newcomers gathered around Elizabeth's father and brothers, the two youngest members of the delegation searched the hall and then made haste to their table.

Elizabeth's mother entered the hall from the kitchens, smiling at the new arrivals. "Oh my, who are all these lovely bairns?"

Phil stood up and shouted, "Herry. Come eat with us. You'll love it here."

"I like Castle Curanta," Herry said, "but this castle is bigger." His big eyes searched the hall, taking in all the tables and the large hearth at one end. "*Much* bigger."

Sabina toddled along behind him, and Elizabeth dipped down and picked her up, giving her a big squeeze before kissing the top of her head. The wee lassie looked up at her, then pointed to Gil, her expression full of a sadness that nearly ripped a hole in Elizabeth's heart and asked, "Ebeth, you and Gil leave me?"

"We had to leave for a short while, but we're back now. Do not worry."

Herry edged closer to Sabina and took her hand, "She's afraid you'll marry and leave her."

"What?" Elizabeth asked, looking over at Gil. They hadn't decided exactly where they were going to live yet. In fact, she feared that discussion so much that she had intentionally not brought it up yet.

Phil and Daw got to their feet and joined the other bairns. "'Tis what we all wonder. Are you moving into Clan Grant and leaving us all at Castle Curanta?'

Sabina's thumb popped into her mouth and she sucked loud enough to be heard across the hall.

Elizabeth's mother took it all in, a look of pride on her face. "Elizabeth, could I talk with you for a moment, please?"

"Of course," she said, standing up and touching each of the bairns in front of her. "I'll be back. I promise. Gil will play the game of hide the rock in the hall."

She had no idea what her mother wanted to speak with her about, but it seemed likely it had to do with the impending nuptials. They hadn't talked much about them, having planned out only the timing and the feast that would accompany it.

Her mother led her into the empty solar. Once the door was closed behind them, her mother asked, "Have you decided where you and Gil will live after your marriage yet?"

Elizabeth sank into the closest chair, taken off-guard by this question. "We haven't discussed it yet, but I would like to stay here to help you and Papa and Kyla manage everything."

"Oh, piddle," her mother said, and Elizabeth didn't have any idea how to answer that. She'd expected her mother to be relieved. "Elizabeth, we will not ignore you if you leave. I know your fears. I know the mistakes I made thinking you were too young to understand, but it shouldn't affect what you do now."

"But Mama, you need me."

Her mother sat down next to her and took her hands in hers. "We love you dearly, and would be broken-hearted if you went verra far, but I think we could survive if you were as close as Castle Curanta. But are *you* ready to leave Clan Grant? That may be the question."

She jumped out of her chair and threw her arms around her mother, breaking into sobs, her breath hitching as she buried her face in her mother's shoulder. "Mama, I don't know what I should do…"

"Listen to me, Elizabeth." She gently maneuvered her back into the chair and Elizabeth had to force herself to take deep breaths to slow her tears. "When I saw you with the wee ones out there in our great hall, who have already missed you and Gil, I see your calling. You are so wonderful with bairns, especially the orphans, I think you belong at Castle Curanta. And the fact that you met your husband while you were doing the Lord's work with the orphans tells me that you are meant for it. Do you not see how much they need you at Castle Curanta?"

She swiped at her tears. "Do you truly think 'tis my calling?"

"I think 'tis the special talent you were given, and 'tis one you should share with the world."

She paused to gather her thoughts, her mind returning to that moment with Maggie, all those years ago, when she'd talked about everyone having a special talent. She'd wondered what hers might be and felt inadequate when she never discovered an innate ability like her sisters possessed.

Was her mother right? Was caring for orphans her special talent?

"Mama, what do you think your special talent is?" She had her own thoughts on this, but she wished to hear her mother's thoughts.

Her mother shrugged and said, "I have a couple of thoughts, but I think one of them is creating my storybooks. I love telling stories to the bairns of our clan."

"I agree, Mama. Wholeheartedly. But your other?"

She took a deep sigh and said, "Loving your sire. It took patience and love for him to build this clan. Mostly his doing, but I'm a part of it, too."

Elizabeth bolted out of her chair and threw her arms around her mother. "Oh, Mama. You're so right."

"About your sire?"

"That, too. But I do belong at Castle Curanta. I promise to visit frequently."

When she opened the door, she was surprised to find Phil and Daw standing there, wide grins on their faces. They whirled around and announced in unison, "They're living at Castle Curanta."

Ignoring the two and their obvious eavesdropping, she strode straight over to Gil and said, "Gil, I'd like to live at Castle Curanta, if you wouldn't mind."

He grinned and said, "Whatever pleases you, love. I'll agree."

The bairns applauded and shouted their excitement.

The wedding took place a sennight later, mostly because her father didn't want anyone thinking Elizabeth was still available.

She was most decidedly not. The day began with a heavy mist over the area, but by midday, the sun peeked out through the clouds. Her mother called up the stairs to her, "Elizabeth, are you ready yet? Your father is coming with the others."

Elizabeth looked at her sisters and whispered, "Well? How do I look?"

"Splendid!" Maeve said.

Kyla kissed her cheek, careful not to touch her hair. Lily had come in with her daughters, Lise and Liliana, and they'd arranged her hair, entwining flowers and ribbons with the long waves that hung down her back.

"Looks much better than that creation you made at MacTear's," Kyla said with a grin. "How could you forget to take that out after it was all over?"

"I forgot." She lifted her eyebrows. "I was more worried about my betrothed and whether Papa had survived the sword fight and the boiling oil than about my hair."

Kyla's grin widened. "Just teasing you. You look absolutely gorgeous, sister."

Her dress was a pastel blue, the cut and color a perfect match for her. Two others would be wearing the same gown today. She looked down at one of them, reaching a hand to her. "Are you ready, daughter?"

Sabina giggled and nodded, smoothing her dress exactly as Elizabeth had.

She and Gil had decided to adopt Sabina so she'd never have any fears of losing them again. The lassie had taken to sleeping in Elizabeth's chamber at Grant Castle until after the wedding. Their cottage was being worked on back at Castle Curanta. They'd decided to add two chambers to it, hoping to fill it with another bairn before long.

They moved down the steps, Kyla and Maeve helping her with the long skirt, but she nearly came to a stop when she saw their mother in the great hall. "Mama, that color is perfect for you."

"Just as it is on you," her mother said with a wide smile. For she was the third person in a pastel blue gown.

Once they reached the bottom of the stairs, Sabina rushed over to hug her new grandmother, giggling. When she ended the hug, she stood between mother and daughter, a look of wonder on her face.

Elizabeth knelt down and kissed her wee lassie's cheek. "And you are lovely, as well, daughter. You have fun staying with Grandmama this eve." Sabina giggled, the same way she did whenever Elizabeth called her daughter—which was why she did it so often.

"Aye, Mama."

Oh, how she loved being called Mama by Sabina, a sound that was the sweetest music of all.

The door opened, so they turned around, and a gasp escaped Elizabeth at the sight that came through the door. First her father, looking splendid in his dress plaid, followed by her three brothers, Jamie, Jake, and Connor.

"All is arranged for you, lass," her father said. "You look lovely." He kissed her cheek, then Maddie's. "You all do."

Behind them came the four cousins, all in their finest: Alasdair, Alick, and Elshander, with Dyna following them in.

"You all look so wonderful," Elizabeth said, directing her comment to her nephews and niece, but then she stepped onto her tiptoes to kiss her sire's cheek and whisper to him how special he looked.

"We made Dyna come in last," Alick said while Els giggled.

Dyna just smirked and waited, as if she were only allowing them to think it a victory. Knowing her canny mind, Elizabeth thought that was probably true.

"This is the way we will travel to the chapel," her father said. "No horses, we're walking today. So everyone may turn around, and this is the order in which we'll travel."

They all did as instructed, Alex, Maddie, and Elizabeth in the back. Kyla and Maeve fell in on either side of Sabina, just in front of Elizabeth. The brothers traveled in front of the women. The cousins in front of the brothers.

And in the very front? Dyna, who turned her head enough to

look at the three boys and say a quick, "Hmmph."

Jake said, "Will they never learn who the quickest is?"

Connor just laughed.

The door to the great hall was opened, held by Loki and Finlay, and they exited in order. As soon as they reached the bottom steps, a group of orphans carrying flowers surrounded their group.

All was quiet as the members of the clan lined the path, watching the group head to the chapel, mothers holding linen squares to mop up their tears. The onlookers followed as the group continued on to the chapel in the farthest corner of the bailey. The cousins tried to tell Dyna which way to go, but she ignored them, choosing the best route herself, judging mostly by the mass of observers.

The wedding group arrived at the chapel, and Elizabeth gasped as soon as she saw Gil.

She had to bite back tears, reminding herself that this was the happiest day of her life, not the saddest. But he was so devastatingly handsome in his leine and Grant dress plaid that it nearly left her speechless. Her sire and mother kissed her cheek before they found their seats inside the chapel, and the rest of the group moved to the back, leaving only Gil and Loki, and Elizabeth and Kyla in the front.

Gil held his elbow out to her and she took it, squeezing him just a wee bit, though she truly wanted to pinch herself.

Here she was, every single part of her dream coming true. Marrying the man she adored in front of her parents and family, in front of the daughter they'd taken into their home, and soon they would move to Castle Curanta, where she and Gil would join Loki and Bella in caring for all the orphans they found.

She glanced up at her husband, and he smiled at her. This was a familiar smile, the one that meant she shouldn't worry about everything. Here he was, her rock, her love, her everything. The man who could show her the stars but help her deal with life when it turned confusing. The man who was more grounded in his life than she was, something that was a surprise because he'd been an orphan himself, treated worse than any person should be forced to endure.

Yet here he was, stronger than anyone, the kind of person who could be counted on forever, and he'd chosen to be by *her* side.

And that meant more than anything.

CHAPTER TWENTY-FOUR

ALL HAD GONE perfectly. The weather had been kind, the food had been delicious, and the dancing had been delightful. When Gil twirled her the first time, she leaned over and whispered, "How did I not know you could dance like this, husband?"

"I've been saving it all for you," he said, waggling his brow at her.

They clapped and danced, shouted and kissed, hugged and ate too much, but it was perfect. When they finally arrived back at their seats at the dais, she said, "Do you think our cottage will be ready soon?"

"Loki said not until a day or two more. I think we'll have to sleep here. I don't think either of us will be ready to ride to Castle Curanta this eve. Do you?"

"Nay, it's just..." she leaned over to whisper. "You know how loud I can be."

He nuzzled her ear and said, "That I do, but I'll do my best to smother your shouts."

There was only one part of the marriage left that concerned her. Everything had gone beautifully, even the weather cooperating to make the day special. All that was left was their wedding night.

Fortunately, she'd never heard of anyone checking the linens the morning after in her clan. She'd heard of some lairds who practiced the ridiculous custom of hanging the blood-stained sheets out the window as proof of the bride's maidenhead still being intact, but she'd never heard of it being practiced for any of her close family. Not with the Ramsays, the Camerons, or the Drummonds. In fact, she nearly snorted at the possibility of Diana of Drummond allowing such a practice.

If her mother or sire wished to check, she'd be horrified. In fact, the thought had crossed her mind that perhaps she should prick her skin with a needle to leave blood on the linens.

But where would they spend the night?

The thought of staying in the castle horrified her because she knew their lovemaking could be quite noisy. It was her own voice that she needed to silence, not Gil's.

So it came as quite a relief when her parents approached them on the dais and her mother whispered, "We have a surprise for you. We've found a cottage for you to spend your night together. Your sire will lead you there. Cook has prepared a lovely basket of food and wine. We cleaned the cottage and placed all new linens inside. Your father cut wood, so there's plenty for the hearth to keep you warm. No one else knows where it is, so 'twill be quite private for you. And you needn't worry about Sabina. We're overjoyed to watch her."

Elizabeth looked to her husband, pleased to see the approval on his face.

"If you agree," her mother explained, "I have your best riding clothes in the kitchens for you to change into, and I packed a couple of bags for you. Even your favorite soap."

"Mama, that sounds wonderful. Gil?" she asked, looking up at him. "What say you?"

He gave her hand a squeeze under the table and said, "Sounds perfect. Shall we go now before it turns wild here?"

She nodded, then gave Gil a kiss on his cheek so she could sneak into the kitchens and change out of her gown. Her gown was beautiful, but she didn't wish to ruin it riding a horse, so she was pleased her mother had thought ahead.

A short time later, they were riding away from Grant Castle on their horses, she and Gil riding separately because they had supplies for the horses to carry. They'd managed to sneak away without being seen, for which she was grateful. "Papa, did you tell my brothers to keep the crowd at bay?"

"I did," he said. "I remember another golden-haired lass who blushed every time someone mentioned the words 'wedding night' around her, so I wished to keep the drunken guests away from you. I know how delicate your mother was about it. Though I think you are of stronger constitution than your mother was when we were married, I wished to spare you the embarrassment."

"I would agree with you, Papa. Mama is still verra shy at heart. 'Tis her nature."

"Aye, unless someone threatens a bairn of hers or a grandbairn, she is shy. Or any bairn for that matter." He spurred his horse into a gallop, and they followed him, sailing across the meadow and in the light of dusk.

It was a beautiful ride. There was little wind, but the sun was nearly down, the pink clouds making it quite a view this eve.

She pointed to the horizon and said, "'Tis a most perfect sunset for our wedding day, Gil."

So entranced with the view of the sun dropping in the sky, she didn't pay any attention to the route, instead blindly following her sire until he led them down a path that wound through the thick forest.

An area that was more than vaguely familiar.

They were headed to their cottage.

Theirs!

Her father stopped his horse in front of the cottage they'd been using for five moons now. She said nothing as they dismounted and tied up the horses, reminding herself that if anyone had come upon it, they would have no way of knowing that she and Gil had fixed it and made it usable.

In fact, though she'd brought linens and furs there, she'd taken care that none of them could be traced back to her. They were all cast-offs from the cellars, threadbare from use but still suitable for their adventures.

She said nothing. Gil gave her a glance after her sire dismounted that served as a warning. His look told her their thoughts were in exact alignment. The others had no way of knowing this was their cottage, and it would be best to keep it that way.

"'Tis a fine area," Gil said, his voice remarkably steady. "Are you sure 'tis unused?"

Her father said, "Kyla found it after the betrothal, so Mama has been out here adding her feminine touches. She and Maeve cleaned and spruced it up with new coverings for the windows. No one has been here that we've seen."

Once they stepped inside, she couldn't help but gasp. "'Tis lovely. Oh, Papa, Mama and Maeve did a lovely job." Fresh rushes on the floor added a fine odor of heather to the air. There were new thick fur coverings on the windows and dried flowers had been added to the hearth mantle. New blankets sat in a basket by the hearth, and the bed had a brand new covering, a beautiful shade of blue.

Her father set the basket of food on the table and banked the fire. He checked the urns and pitchers, full of fresh water. He pointed to the basket. "Aunt Jennie and Uncle Aedan sent a nice bottle of wine from France. And there's plenty of ale, too."

He strode over to her and clasped her shoulders. "I'm pleased to see you so happy, lass. I wish you a lifetime of joy." He kissed her cheek, then clasped Gil's shoulder. "Take good care of my lassie. If you need anything, let me know."

They followed him to the door, watching him mount his horse and turn it toward them.

He was about to leave, but then stopped, turning back to face them. "Gil, I have one more question for you. When you return, would you mind building me a chair as large as the one you made inside?"

"It would be my honor, my laird," Gil said immediately.

Elizabeth squeezed his hand, trying to tell him to stop, but one look at her poor husband told her he'd already recognized his error.

They'd been skillfully caught.

They both stared at her father, waiting for his response, but he just winked. Then, with a grin, he said, "Glad to see you kept enough wood cut to keep her warm. A true sign you'll take good care of my lassie."

THE END

DEAR READER,

Thanks for reading! As you can see, this is Book 12 in The Highland Clan, a series that has no ending in sight. There is such a slew of characters to pull from that I will never end it!

Next up is a trilogy or tetralogy of healers—Brigid, Tara, Jennet, and possibly another, though I'm not sure who the fourth will be.

So for our next adventure, I'm excited to be heading back to Ramsay land.

Happy reading,

Keira Montclair

keiramontclair@gmail.com
www.keiramontclair.com
www.facebook.com/KeiraMontclair
www.pinterest.com/KeiraMontclair

OTHER NOVELS BY KEIRA MONTCLAIR

THE CLAN GRANT SERIES

#1- RESCUED BY A HIGHLANDER-
Alex and Maddie
#2- HEALING A HIGHLANDER'S HEART-
Brenna and Quade
#3- LOVE LETTERS FROM LARGS-
Brodie and Celestina
#4-JOURNEY TO THE HIGHLANDS-
Robbie and Caralyn
#5-HIGHLAND SPARKS-
Logan and Gwyneth
#6-MY DESPERATE HIGHLANDER-
Micheil and Diana
#7-THE BRIGHTEST STAR IN THE HIGHLANDS-
Jennie and Aedan
#8- HIGHLAND HARMONY-
Avelina and Drew

THE HIGHLAND CLAN

LOKI-Book One
TORRIAN-Book Two
LILY-Book Three
JAKE-Book Four
ASHLYN-Book Five
MOLLY-Book Six
JAMIE AND GRACIE- Book Seven
SORCHA-Book Eight
KYLA-Book Nine
BETHIA-Book Ten
LOKI'S CHRISTMAS STORY-Book Eleven

ELIZABETH-Book Twelve

<u>THE BAND OF COUSINS</u>

HIGHLAND VENGEANCE
HIGHLAND ABDUCTION
HIGHLAND RETRIBUTION
HIGHLAND LIES
HIGHLAND FORTITUDE
HIGHLAND RESILIENCE
HIGHLAND DEVOTION
HIGHLAND BRAWN
HIGHLAND YULETIDE MAGIC

<u>HIGHLAND SWORDS</u>

THE SCOT'S BETRAYAL
THE SCOT'S SPY
THE SCOT'S PURSUIT
THE SCOT'S QUEST
THE SCOT'S DECEPTION
THE SCOT'S ANGEL

<u>THE SOULMATE CHRONICLES</u>

#1 TRUSTING A HIGHLANDER
#2 TRUSTING A SCOT

<u>STAND-ALONE BOOKS</u>

THE BANISHED HIGHLANDER
REFORMING THE DUKE-REGENCY
WOLF AND THE WILD SCOTS
FALLING FOR THE CHIEFTAIN-
3RD in a collaborative trilogy

<u>THE SUMMERHILL SERIES-</u>
<u>CONTEMPORARY ROMANCE</u>

#1-ONE SUMMERHILL DAY
#2-A FRESH START FOR TWO
#3-THREE REASONS TO LOVE

ABOUT THE AUTHOR

KEIRA MONTCLAIR IS the pen name of an author who lives in South Carolina with her husband. She loves to write fast-paced, emotional romance, especially with children as secondary characters.

When she's not writing, she loves to spend time with her grandchildren. She's worked as a high school math teacher, a registered nurse, and an office manager. She loves ballet, mathematics, puzzles, learning anything new, and creating new characters for her readers to fall in love with.

She writes historical romantic suspense. Her bestselling series is a family saga that follows two medieval Scottish clans through four generations and now numbers over thirty books.

Contact her through her website,
www.keiramontclair.com.

Printed in the USA
CPSIA information can be obtained
at www.ICGtesting.com
LVHW020246280424
778676LV00024B/519

9 781947 213708